Her Valentine Surprise

Manhattan Holiday Loves, Book 2

By

AYLA ASHER

Contents

Cover Design: Angela Haddon Book Cover Design

Because the author was craving a super-sweet HEA with an inexperienced hero. I mean, it's Valentine's Day, ladies. Enjoy!

Chapter 1

J oy Paulson sat at her desk, appearing to finish the memo her boss had dictated earlier. To the casual onlooker, she was hard at work—a diligent executive assistant with fingers that typed a hundred and twenty words a minute with ease. But Joy's mind was a million miles away from the task at hand. Currently, she was watching her boss out of the corner of her eye, attempting not to squirm in her chair.

Drake Blevins was doing curls with the dumbbell set he kept in his office.

Like he did every day at two p.m.

And her heart was a quivering pile of slush.

Giving an indecipherable sigh, Joy told herself to stop being an idiot and focus on work. The memo needed to go out at two-thirty, so she only had a few minutes to perfect it. Her OCD would accept nothing less.

Zeroed in on the screen, she didn't sense Drake by her side until he slipped his hand over her shoulder. Gasping, she flinched and gazed up at him.

"Oh, you startled me."

"Sorry, Joy. Didn't mean to scare you," Drake said. "How's the memo coming along?"

She gave him a smile, hoping he didn't notice how her cheeks warmed like a bumbling dolt. "Great. I'll be done in five and you can look it over before I send it out."

He squeezed her shoulder, causing her heart to slam into over-drive. "Thanks. Just email it to me when you're ready."

"Will do," she said, giving a salute, and then realized how stupid that was. Could she ever act like a normal human being in front of him? Most likely not, since he was hands-down the hottest man she'd ever laid eyes on. Dark, thick hair, piercing blue eyes, broad shoulders—he was basically the next James Bond, if they were open to auditions.

He strolled back to his office, leaving Joy at her desk outside his slightly ajar door. Muttering that she was going to crawl into a hole and never return, she resumed typing. She was almost finished with the last sentence when the computer froze.

"No!" she said in a hushed whisper, frantically hitting the 'enter' key. The screen just stared back, the tiny blue circle buffering, the monitor frozen in a sea of hazy white.

Anxiety clutched at her throat, choking her, and she told herself to calm down. Inhaling several deep breaths, she lifted the handle of the phone beside her desk and called IT.

"IT Department, Sam speaking."

"Sam," she said, relief evident in her tone. He was her favorite IT team member and probably one of the nicest men on the planet. If anyone could help her, it would be Sam. "You've got to help me. My computer's on the fritz again and I have to complete this memo, like, five minutes ago."

There was a brief pause. "Joy?"

"Yes, it's me. Please, Sam. I need you desperately."

He cleared his throat. "Sure thing. I'll be there in one minute."

Biting her lip with worry, she waited for him. He approached, his tall frame draped in the black pants and polo shirt that all the IT professionals wore. When he stopped at her side, he smiled and Joy took stock of his teeth. They were the straightest she'd ever seen.

"It would be better if you let me sit in the chair," he said, his voice deep and warm.

"Oh," she said, shaking her head and jumping up. "Please, sit." She gestured to the chair and he lowered into it, eyebrows drawing together as he assessed the screen.

"I thought Drake was getting you a new computer," he said, clicking the mouse as he moved it over the pad. "This one's ancient. All he has to do is approve the form online and I'll install it for you."

Joy shrugged. "I guess he hasn't had time. We've been so busy with the sneaker campaign and the women's razor promotion. Drake's main goal is maintaining the firm's status as the number one ad agency in Manhattan. My new computer is probably the last thing on his list."

She watched Sam's fingers rove over the keys, noting how long they were, his hands broad. He was tall—she guessed him at least six-feet, four-inches, so it would make sense he had large hands. Did that mean he had a large...?

Giving her head a quick shake, she cut off the drifting thoughts. His hands worked magic over the keyboard, opening all sorts of windows and typing prompts. Two minutes later, he swiveled away from the desk and grinned up at her.

"All done. I deleted some of your temporary files and cleaned things up a bit. It should run faster and stop freezing, for now. Tell Drake to approve that new workstation, STAT, and I'll get it up and running for you."

"You're a lifesaver!" she cried, squeezing his shoulder. "Thank you so much, Sam."

His gaze drifted to her hand, lingering for a bit, before lifting to hers. "Sure. I'd do anything for you, Joy. You're the nicest person we have in this joint." Standing, he gave her another deep smile. "Call me anytime. See ya." Placing his hands in his pockets, he ambled down the hallway lined with cubicles.

"He really is so sweet," Joy murmured, lips curving as she finished the memo and sent it to Drake for approval. Deciding she needed to buy him a coffee tomorrow, she said a silent prayer of thanks to Sam Davidson for saving her ass, yet again.

S am Davidson walked through the office, back to the dungeon that housed the IT department. He worked there with his buddies, Will, Jamal and Frank. They'd all become tight since Sam came on board two years ago, and lovingly referred to their hidden back room as the "forgotten lair." The IT department was the unsung hero of the marketing firm, but that was fine with Sam. He'd always been burdened with terrible shyness and preferred the solitary existence.

"Do me a favor and send the form for a new workstation to Drake again, will ya?" he asked his supervisor, Frank. "He was supposed to fill it out for Joy two months ago. Her computer's on its last leg."

"You got it, man," Frank said, giving him a thumbs up.

They were basically a foursome of loners, quiet and obsessed with all things tech, but it created an inherent camaraderie be-tween them. Every once in a while, Sam would meet up with them on a Friday night to play cards. They were nice guys and could always fall into a discussion on gaming or something else that would totally be considered geek-worthy.

Sitting at his desk, Sam inhaled a deep breath, commanding his heartbeat to chill the fuck out. When Joy had touched his shoulder, he'd almost lost it. She'd smiled down at him with those gorgeous, full lips and her adorable heart-shaped face had such genuine sincerity. Her light-blue eyes had latched onto his and he'd had to physically shift in her chair. Closing his lids, he imag-ined, for one moment, strumming his fingers through her straw-berry-blond hair. It always smelled so damn good, like flowers and rain, and he'd love nothing more than to rub his cheek against it as he inhaled the fragrance.

Lifting his lids, he commanded his overactive imagination to shut it down. Wasting time thinking about a girl whom you had zero chance with was the definition of futility. Sam was practical and didn't enjoy the frivolity of spending time on things that were never going to happen. After all, Joy was in love with Drake. It was obvious to anyone who observed them interact. Sam understood why, of course. Drake was the definition of what women wanted in today's modern dating world. His foster sister, Sarah, had shown him enough of her alpha male romance novels that he fully understood he was the loser in the story, where Drake was the dashing hero.

How categorically unfair, yet unalterable all the same.

Sighing, he got to work on the ticket that popped up on his screen. Whether Joy was in love with Drake or someone else, she would never fall in love with him. For, Sam had a secret he carried inside, wrapped in a hefty dose of annoyance and a slight bit of embarrassment.

Yes, Sam had been in love with Joy for almost two years now.

But he'd been a virgin for twenty-nine years.

Even if he had the balls to ask her out, which he didn't, he wouldn't know how to make love to her. The disconcertment washed over him and he straightened in his chair, attempting to push the thoughts away. He would have no idea how to make her moan...or how to elicit a cry from her pretty lips...or how to excite her until she called his name, pleading for him to make her come.

No, sadly, Sam had no idea how to accomplish any of those things.

And that was why he would carry on with his secret love for Joy and hope she found someone who could please her in all the ways he so desperately wanted to, but never could.

Telling himself to move the hell on, he resumed working on the open IT request, shoulders hunched over his desk. It was going to be a long afternoon.

Chapter 2

O nce the memo had been sent through the ether, Joy felt she could breathe. Relaxing at her desk, she took out her phone to text her two best friends, Laura and Kayla.

Joy: Crisis averted at work. The super-sweet IT guy saved my ass, yet again. Job saved and I can keep working with Captain Hotness.

Joy laughed at her friend's response.

Laura: Sounds exciting. Maybe get the hot boss and the IT guy to stay late and rock your world together. One of us needs to have a threesome before we all get hitched and Kayla's out since she's in looooooove.

Kayla: While I am in love, I'm pretty sure Carter won't propose until we're eighty. That seems about the right amount of time for him to get over his fear of the M-word.

Joy: It will happen, K. Sending you good vibes. Gotta go.

She texted them a kiss emoji and read the email that had just popped up. It was from Drake, explaining he'd like to meet with her in his office at five-thirty after everyone left for the day. Her eyebrows drew together and she wondered why. Thrumming pulses coursed blood through her veins as she stared at the email. It was probably nothing. Maybe he wanted to follow up on the memo, or something else benign. Shrugging off the silly reaction, she wrote him back telling him that was fine.

The day wound down and everyone headed home. Joy glanced over her shoulder to see Drake on the phone, his long legs atop the desk, crossed at the ankles. His Italian loafers seemed to shine and Joy wondered how often he polished them.

The office was quiet as she knocked on Drake's door a few minutes later.

"Hey," she said, tentatively walking in. "You ready for me?"

His expression turned slightly suggestive. "Always. Come on in."

Leaving the door open, she sat in one of the open leather seats in front of his desk. His direct blue gaze flitted over her and she smoothed her hands over her skirt. "So, what did you want to meet about?"

He leaned forward, resting his elbows on the desk. "I don't want to come across as inappropriate, Joy, but I reached out to HR today."

Her heartbeat quickened. "Did I do something wrong?"

His lips curved. "On the contrary, I've found myself thinking about you...*romantically*...the past few weeks. I'm a direct person, Joy, and don't feel like wasting time. I called HR to see if it would violate any of our policies for me to ask you on a date. They said that as long as you and I complete their inter-office relationship forms, we're totally in the clear. So, I guess what I'm asking is," he held up two fingers, ticking them off as he spoke, "one, would you like to go on a date with me and, two, if so, will you complete the forms?" Giving her one of his epically handsome smiles, he slid a small stack of papers across his desk toward her.

Joy couldn't have been more floored. Struggling to keep her jaw from falling to the ground, she reached for the papers, studying them since she found it impossible to maintain eye contact with him. Of course, she'd imagined Drake asking her out a thousand times, but never quite like this. There was something so...*cold* about it.

Lifting her irises to his, she said, "Well, first of all, I'm extremely flattered, Drake. I do find myself quite attracted to you."

He gave a smug shrug of his shoulders. "I figured. Ladies usually say I'm easy on the eyes."

Um, okay. Arrogant much? Feeling her brow furrow slightly, she forged on. "I'd be happy to think about it, but I'm not sure I want to go down the road of getting HR involved."

"Well, we could always keep it secret, but I don't think that's a good idea. In the end, if it ends badly, I'd have to fire you." She straightened, giving him an incredulous look. "Kidding, Joy," he said, holding up his hands. "Wow, you're more serious than I've ever seen you."

Standing, he rounded the desk and sat on the edge, reaching down to take her hand. Holding it, he said, "Look, I just want this to be on the up and up. No chance of misunderstandings. I like you, Joy. You're stunning and so damn sweet. I'd really like to take you out, but only if you want to. Why don't you take the paperwork with you and look it over?" He picked up the stack and handed it to her. "Take your time. I'll be here when you're ready."

"Okay," she said, still too shocked to be thrilled, which is what she would've expected when asked out by the man she'd been pining over for years now. Rising, she squeezed his hand. "I appreciate you being so...thorough. I'll think everything over and get back to you in a few days."

"Sounds great." He stood, the pungent smell of his cologne wafting through her nostrils. She'd always liked it but today it seemed overwhelming. Giving him a hesitant smile, she jetted from the office, grabbed her scarf and packed up her belongings.

Heading into the cold early-January evening, she watched her breath form a puff as she tried to wrap her head around what had just occurred. Her hot-as-hell boss had asked her out, which she'd been dreaming about forever. But it had felt like a business transaction more than anything steamy or exciting.

Deciding she needed her two best friends' opinions, she texted them that they were required to join a mandatory video chat session at nine p.m. that evening. No exceptions. Reeling from the bizarre interaction, she decided to walk home, hoping the fresh air would clear her head for twenty-two blocks.

"**I** swear, guys, it was so strange," Joy said later, lying on the couch with her hair fanned over the arm as she spoke into the screen. "Like he didn't really care whether I said yes or no. There was nothing romantic or sexy about it at all. How could something like this happen? It definitely wasn't like this when he asked me out in my fantasies."

"What was it like?" Laura asked, waggling her eyebrows.

"Well," Joy shrugged, "in my dreams, he lifts me in his arms and tells me he can't live another moment until he makes sweet passionate love to me. Then he gently lays me on the bed and gives me a full, twenty-minute foot massage before making me orgasm three times back to back. Then, we bang. I mean, that's pretty normal, right?" She snickered.

"Yeah, that's super-normal," Carter chimed in, leaning in front of Kayla to obstruct her face. "Guys totally have the same fantasy." He rolled his gorgeous brown eyes.

Kayla smushed her hand over his face, pushing him out of the way. "Excuse my overly *rude* boyfriend," she said, giving a cute squeak when he planted a wet kiss on her cheek. "Together less than a year and he still thinks he's god's gift to women."

"Hey," Carter said off-screen. "Take it back. I'm the man of your dreams, woman. Admit it or I'm leaving forever."

"Bye," she said, sticking her tongue out at him.

"My heart is broken, ladies," Carter said, shoving his face toward the screen again. "I'm out. Good luck with the boss man, although he sounds creepy. Don't be long, baby," he said, pecking Kayla on the lips. "I need to remind you why you're the luckiest woman in the world."

"Go away," she said, giving him a good-natured shove. He waved to the screen and trailed out of the room.

"Sorry, guys. Annoying, but so damn hot. I have no willpower."

"I heard that!" Carter yelled from the bedroom.

Laura laughed. "You guys are so cute. I only barfed in my mouth once during that interaction. Now, back to Joy. What are you gonna do, love? Are you going to fill out the forms and let him take you out?"

Joy sighed. "I don't know. I never in a million years thought I'd say no to Drake, but I don't have a good feeling about it for some reason. Maybe I should just chalk it up to the notion that we're supposed to just be coworkers. Well, boss and executive assistant coworkers."

"Yeah, that's what I don't like about it, J," Kayla said. "As an attorney, this raises all sorts of red flags for me. There are so many shades of harassment and coercion here. I don't know, it makes me uneasy."

"But he's so damn hot," Laura whined. "Why are the hot ones always crazy, psychotic or complete jerks? I've dated three duds in the last year, including Brandon. Although I won't blame Kayla for that. Sometimes things aren't meant to be."

Kayla frowned. "I'm really bummed it didn't work out between you guys. I had no idea he was still in love with his ex. Yikes."

"His loss," Laura said. "I'm persistent. Don't worry, ladies. One day, I'll find the man of my dreams. Hope he likes dentures and baby powder because at the rate I'm going, he's going to have to change diapers—and I mean mine, not our kids."

Joy snickered. "I don't know why guys suck so much. Maybe I should consider dating a middle of the road type of guy. Someone who's not oozing sex appeal, but just normal and cute. There is this one guy..."

"Ohhh..." her friends sang in unison.

"Who?" Kayla asked.

"It's nothing, really," she said, shaking her head. "Remember that super-nice IT guy I mentioned at work? His name is Sam. He's not melt-your-panties hot like Drake or Carter—"

"Damn straight!" Carter called from the bedroom.

"I swear, I'm going to lock him in there and throw away the key," Kayla muttered, rolling her eyes.

Joy chuckled. "But he's attractive. Dirty blond hair, piercing hazel eyes and killer straight teeth. You guys know I have a thing with teeth."

"Yep," Laura said. "Who doesn't?"

"Fair," Joy agreed. "He helped fix my computer today and I noticed how large his hands were. Like, really big. It obviously caused me to wonder, well, you know."

"Oh, I know, honey," Laura said. "I need to meet this dude, ASAP. I was spot on about Carter's cock and I need to assess the situation for you. I have a radar for these things."

"One word and the vagina is closed for the night!" Kayla yelled to the bedroom.

"Understood, and I suddenly have laryngitis," Carter called back.

Kayla giggled. "Sorry. So, tell us more about Sam. Maybe he's a better prospect. Are you attracted to him?"

"I'm..." Joy struggled to define her reaction to observing his long fingers move across her keyboard earlier. "Yeah, I actually think I am. Or, I could be at least. But he's super-quiet and a bit shy. I'm not sure he'd have the courage to ask me out."

"Well, it is the twenty-first century, dear. I think it might be okay if you ask him out."

"I, uh, yeah...I guess I could. I don't know, I'm just not even ready to take that on yet. I need to figure out what to do about Drake."

"I say tell him no," Kayla said. "Sorry, J, but as your attorney, which I've now dubbed myself, I just can't advise dating your boss. It would jeopardize too much for you. You've worked really hard at RMG and I don't want to see you have to start over."

"As much as it pains me to say it since he's Idris Elba level hot, I have to say pass, J," Laura said. "I'm really sorry for you *and* your vagina."

Joy sighed, smiling wistfully at her friends. "I think you guys are right. What a bummer. Well, at least I can say I was asked out by a total hottie. I'm kind of in Kayla's league right now."

"Sorry, Joy," Kayla said. "I thought I'd be single forever, but it happened to me. I know it will happen for you."

"You guys know I don't really mind being single. I actually love it. But I'm not opposed to finding someone if it feels right. I'm thirty-two and still have plenty of time."

"True. You're the baby. Kayla and I are grandmas over here at thirty-four."

"But we don't look a day over thirty-three," Kayla joked, chucking her eyebrows.

Joy's laughter filtered through the phone. "I love you guys. Okay, I'll keep you posted."

"On the IT guy's package?" Laura asked. "Absolutely. You gotta get on that, J. Love!" Waving, she disconnected.

Kayla smiled. "Bye, sweetie. You'll figure it out. Text me tomorrow."

"Bye!" Joy called, blowing her a kiss. Settling into the couch, she held the phone to her chest and stared at the ceiling in disbelief. She was going to tell Drake no. Holy hell. Resigned to the knowledge that some things just weren't meant to be, she grabbed the half-eaten carton of ice cream from the fridge and settled for sweet instead of hot. No, her hot, sexy boss was off-limits. Damn. Life just really sucked sometimes.

Chapter 3

The next morning, Joy asked Drake if she could speak to him privately. Once situated in his office, she cleared her throat and began the awkward conversation.

"Drake, I just want to say I'm so flattered you want to go out with me. It's really sweet."

"Great," he said, eyebrows arching. "Do you have the paperwork?"

Joy bit her lip. "I decided not to sign it. Unfortunately, I'm going to have to decline. I think you're a wonderful man but I just don't feel comfortable dating my boss."

His brow furrowed. "Is it the stupid joke I made about firing you? I was kidding."

"I know, and it's not that at all. You're a wonderful person but I just don't feel like I can cross the line of dating someone I work with. I'm really sorry, Drake. I hope you can understand where I'm coming from."

His blue eyes narrowed, and Joy noticed they were laced with anger. Hmmm. Guess he didn't get rejected much, which made sense due to his extreme attractiveness.

"I..." He seemed to be searching for words. Sitting back in his chair, he said, "Well, if that's how you feel, I'll have to accept it. Thanks for letting me know. You can close the door behind you."

Wow, he was pissed. Joy had never seen her usually jovial boss be so curt. Wanting to soothe him, she said, "I hope we can still be friends. I really enjoy—"

"Of course," he said, interrupting her. "I'll have the next dictation to you by lunchtime. Please close the door behind you."

Accepting the rude dismissal, Joy stood and walked back to her desk. As she opened the browser, she realized her hand was shaking as it maneuvered the mouse. Drake was extremely upset and she hadn't expected his vitriolic reaction. Terrified her job was now in jeopardy, she attempted to get to work, knowing that concentration would be fleeting. Sighing, she pulled up the next task on her list and began typing.

S am received a call from Drake around two p.m.

"Sam speaking."

"Hey, it's Drake. My stupid computer is frozen. Can you log in like you did last time and see what's up?"

"Sure," Sam said, opening the connect window. "You'll see a box pop up. Just type in code seven-three-two-nine."

"Done," Drake said and Sam took control of his computer. "Hey, I'm going to head downstairs and get a coffee. I'll be back. Just close out when you're done."

"Sure thing," Sam said. Maneuvering around the screen, he was able to unfreeze the computer. Drake had a ton of files open and Sam began clicking on them to see if he could close any that weren't needed. When he clicked on the open internet browser, an email draft popped up. Sam's eyes immediately darted to Joy's name, and before he could stop himself, he began reading.

Well, remember the bet we had about who could bang our execu-tive assistant first? I asked Joy out and I totally thought she'd say yes. She can't look away when I do curls in the office and I know she wants to fuck me. But she said no, the little bitch. Guess I'm losing this one. How about we go double or nothing on the hottest chick that works in our building? There's this hot one on the third floor who I see every time I get coffee. She'd totally suck my dick. Let me know if you're in. By the way, Joy really pissed me off. I'm going to have to find a way to fire her. Imagine someone like that mousy little twit rejecting me. Whore.

Anyway, about the Knicks game. I can do January twenty-seventh or twenty-eighth...

Sam stopped reading as he struggled to catch his breath. What an asshole. Sam had never had an affinity for Drake since he was arrogant and bossy with the IT department, but he hadn't thought him an outright jerk. Obviously, he was more of a prick than Sam had realized.

Thinking of Joy, he sat back in his chair and threaded his fingers together behind his head. Should he tell her about the email? It was definitely wrong for Sam to have read it, he knew that, but what was done was done. Joy was such an amazing person and he certainly didn't want Drake to target her. Lifting his phone, he snapped a shot of the email, just in case. Reclaiming the mouse, he finished working on Drake's computer and logged out.

Biting his thumbnail—one of his worst and most persistent habits—he debated what to do. First, he should assess whether Joy suspected anything. Probably not, but he didn't want to assume. Rising, he stalked down the hallway, straight to her desk.

"Hey, Sam," she said, pulling the dictation earbuds from her ears. "Did you like the coffee?"

She'd brought him coffee that morning with milk. Since he was lactose intolerant, he couldn't drink it, but he'd never let her know that. Anything Joy did for him was a blessing and he'd humbly accept any table scraps she threw his way, even if they were likely to make him puke his guts out.

"It was fantastic and so thoughtful. Thanks, Joy."

"Sure," she said, beaming up at him, causing a massive thump in his solar plexus. "Thanks for saving my ass and repairing my dinosaur of a computer."

"Anytime," he said. "So, you and Drake were here late last night. I noticed when I was heading out. Is the computer speed making you have to stay late?" He figured that sounded like a good excuse to pry. Right? Hoping she didn't catch on, he continued. "I'll walk into his office right now and have him sign the form for an upgrade if you want me to."

"Oh," she said, her eyebrows drawing together. "I, uh, it was nothing. He asked me to stay late to, um, talk about the memo I sent out yesterday. It's all good. Thank you for checking though. I'm sure he'll get the form to you this week."

Sam wasn't so sure, but he relented. "Okay. I just want you to know I'm here for you if you want to talk or...anything." God, he sounded lame. Feeling his face turn ten shades of red, he said, "You know, 'cause we're friends. At least I hope we are. I'm just a phone call away. You still have my cell, right?" He'd given it to her so she could call him with any laptop issues she experienced at home, although the ulterior motive was just to have her call him anytime. Anywhere. Which he knew would never happen.

"Sure do! I gave you mine, right?"

His eyebrows drew together. "I'm not sure." Pulling his cell out of his pocket, he pulled up the contacts list.

"Oh, I'll just text you then," she said, grabbing her phone and shooting him a text.

Joy: Hi from your favorite office friend.

If she only knew.

"Got it. Okay, I'll leave you alone now. You're probably tired of me stalking you." The minute the words were out of his mouth, he mentally kicked himself. God, he was such an idiot around her. This is why he didn't approach women, and especially women he was helplessly attracted to.

"Oh, a woman needs a good stalker now and then," she teased. "Thanks for checking on me. You're the best." Popping the buds back in her ears, she gave him a dismissive smile.

Right. Time to leave her the hell alone.

As he walked back toward the dungeon, he couldn't shake the feeling he should tell her about Drake's email. However, reading it was a huge breach of privacy and it would violate all sorts of terms of his employment agreement. Feeling caught in a conundrum, he decided he'd think about it for a few days and see what developed.

Chapter 4

By Friday, Joy was thoroughly convinced that Drake was out to fire her. He'd been nasty and cold to her all week and she'd received her first write-up ever. It was for a document Drake had asked to be sent to him by five o'clock on Wednesday. At eleven a.m., he'd sent her an email that he needed it by eleven-thirty. Joy scrambled to finish it and sent it over at eleven thirty-two. That afternoon, Drake had called her into his office.

"I can't have you getting things to me late, Joy," he said from behind his desk as her heart pounded. "If you can't get things to me on time, I'm going to have to find an assistant who can."

"I'm sorry, Drake. You moved up the timeframe and I wanted to ensure it was perfect. You know I'm a bit OCD." It was something they'd joked about in the past, although his expression was devoid of humor.

"I expect it to be perfect *and* on time, Joy. No exceptions. Are we clear?"

Joy swallowed, disbelief coursing through her that their friendly relationship had taken such a turn. "Yes," she said, her voice raspy.

"Good. I'll be writing you up for this. I'll email the documentation to you. Two more strikes and you're out. I'd tread carefully."

Terror slammed her since she desperately needed to remain employed. "Okay," she said, licking her parched lips. "Is this because of the date, Drake? If it is, I just want to say that I'm really sorry—"

"Oh, I'd already forgotten about that," he said in a nasty tone. "Now, if you'll excuse me, I have the conference call with Circle Tires in five minutes. You can shut the door behind you."

Wow. How had she not seen what a prick he was? Feeling like a fool for ever being attracted to him, she'd struggled to retain her composure. As the anxiety attack closed in, she rushed toward the lobby and into the nearby stairwell. The air was cool and Joy collapsed on the stair, burying her face in her hands. How the hell had this happened? Telling herself to remain calm, she took a few minutes before returning to her desk.

Now that it was Friday afternoon, she felt almost ready to breathe a sigh of relief. Drake had been tied up in meetings most of the day and she'd barely had any interaction with him. As she began packing her things to head home, a new email popped up. Opening it, her mouth fell open in shock.

Dear Joy,

It is with great regret that I send you the second and third write-ups this week. One is for the lingerie company memo, which had three typos. The other is for the PowerPoint presentation that was missing three slides. Unfortunately, these errors are unacceptable and I have no choice but to terminate your employment. HR has been notified and they will be emailing you final documents.

Sure enough, another email popped up from HR. Quickly scrolling through it, Joy saw an attachment detailing her termination and another describing her six-week package. Six weeks? Most people at the firm got at least three month's severance when they were fired. Rage consumed her and she stood, turning to glare at Drake through his office window.

"That son of a bitch," she murmured. Stalking into his office, she closed the door so she could give him a piece of her mind.

His expression stopped her cold. "I wouldn't cause a scene if I were you, Joy. Everyone can see us through my office windows. If you treat me with any sort of disrespect, HR has assured me that I can rescind the small severance you were granted."

"How dare you?" she asked, approaching his desk and leaning her palms on the surface. "Because I wouldn't *date* you? This is ridiculous! We've worked together for years, Drake. You know how methodical I am. There is no way there were any mistakes in my work. You must've altered it. I can't believe it," she said, shaking her head. "I never expected this from you."

He gave a deferent shrug. "I'm the big fish around here. You should know that by now. I keep this company thriving and I do that by getting what I want. Unfortunately, your services are no longer needed." He picked up his office phone and tapped on the keypad. "Security? We have an employee who needs to be escorted out." Hanging up the receiver, he gave her a cruel smile. "I'd say you have about one minute to pack up, Joy. I'd get to it."

Joy had to clench her fists to keep from scratching his eyeballs out. For two seconds, she imagined thrusting the letter opener on his desk into his jugular. Then, she gathered her wits. If there was one thing Joy reveled in, it was being a scrapper. And she was smart. Smarter than this jerk.

Pivoting, she headed to her desk. With fast hands, she managed to send her personal email as many things as she could: the documents that were supposedly flawed, the emails she and Drake had exchanged with the differing timelines, the HR package and everything else. Suddenly, a security guard loomed over her and Drake's voice said from behind, "That's enough, Joy. You no longer have access to the computer. Please pack up and leave."

Humiliation washed over her as she collected her possessions, tears burning her eyes. Once she'd gathered her belongings, she glanced up to find everyone watching in disbelief. Sam stood with the other IT guys, his kind hazel eyes filled with concern. Giving him a warbled smile, she accompanied the security guard to the lobby. Once outside, in the cold January air, she crumpled to one of the benches and buried her face in her hands. Pouring out tears of disbelief, she wondered how in the hell something like this could happen.

After witnessing the kerfuffle between Joy and Drake, Sam had two visceral reactions. First, he wanted to follow Joy, pull her into his arms and soothe her until she never cried again. Second, he wanted to smash Drake's face in. Understanding the second option would most likely land him in jail, he headed toward the elevator, frantically pushing the button to summon the elevator.

It was Friday afternoon and the elevator traffic was high. When the doors finally slid open, he tapped his foot as he was whooshed twenty floors to the main lobby. Once there, he jogged outside, desperately searching for her. He finally located her as she was hailing a taxi. The yellow car pulled up and she tucked inside, but not before he saw the tears glistening on her cheeks in the winter sunlight.

Crap. He should've told her about Drake's email. Hell, he should've sent it to HR. Although it would've probably gotten him fired, it was better than Joy experiencing any pain. Sam would most likely cut off his own arm if it meant Joy would give him one of her breathtaking smiles.

Breathing a curse, he headed back inside, determined to help the girl he loved pick up the pieces and move on. He felt responsible for not outing Drake and had an obligation to repair what he'd inadvertently broken. He didn't know how, but he wouldn't stop until he made things right. That was a fucking promise.

Chapter 5

J oy sat on the couch, her two friends blanketing each side. As she sniffed into her tissue, she could almost hear Laura's teeth grinding.

"I swear to god, that fucking bastard. I'm going to find him and throw acid on his perfect face. And then I'm going to hack into his email and send his mother pictures of dicks and tell her they're his."

Joy couldn't help but laugh. "Remind me to never piss you off."

"It's a bad idea, for sure. I'm fucking vicious."

"You did the right thing forwarding all the documentation to your personal email. You're so damn smart, Joy. I'm going to get everything to my friend who specializes in employment law and we're going to fight this with everything we've got."

"I really appreciate that, Kayla," Joy said, blowing her nose, "but I can't afford a lawyer. Now that I don't have a job, I can barely afford anything. Since we sold the house to pay for Mom's assisted living, I don't have anywhere to go. Corinne is in Atlanta, for Christ's sakes," she said, referencing her sister. "What am I going to do?"

"First of all, Kevin will totally work on contingency, so don't worry about that at all."

"I don't want to be that client who doesn't pay—"

"Stop it, J," Kayla said. "There's no discussion on that. He owes me one anyway. And as far as getting a new job, we'll help you look.

Laura and I have a ton of connections and we won't stop until you find something."

"I should've gotten my bachelor's degree," Joy said, her chin warbling. "Since I never finished it, my options are so limited. I earned eighty-seven thousand dollars a year at RMG. Their pay was second-to-none. Most firms only pay fifty or sixty at best. I can't survive on that, especially with Mom's bills too."

"Did that bastard know you've been supporting your mother for years?" Laura asked. "Because if he did, I'll most likely just Lorena Bobbitt him. No man who fires a woman who financially supports her sick mother should be allowed to live with a fully intact penis."

Joy breathed a laugh. "I mentioned it to him, here and there, but we never had any in-depth discussions about it. He didn't realize I dropped out of college to enter the workforce because Mom's medical bills were so exorbitant. It was one of the reasons I strived to do everything perfectly, so I could get the highest percentage of every pay raise opportunity."

"God, this is so many shades of fucked up," Kayla said. "We're totally fighting this. In the meantime, I need you to know we're here for you. I make a shit ton of money at the firm now and Carter's play is about to open on Broadway. He thinks he might get nominated for a Tony on this one. I'm not saying that to brag, but to let you know we have money that we are more than willing to share with you. You're my family and it would be an honor to support you through this."

"And we all know my parents are loaded," Laura said with a sardonic shrug, "so my trust fund is your trust fund."

Joy encircled both their wrists, squeezing with all the love she felt for her two amazing best friends. "I really appreciate that, guys, but I can't take your charity."

"I swear to god, J," Kayla said. "I won't even hear an argument on this. I'm a lawyer. I debate every day. You're going to lose this battle. Don't even try to fight me on this."

Sighing, Joy nodded, realizing it was futile to try and sway them. Although she'd never take money from either of them, it was best to let them believe she was open to it. She was proud, maybe too much so, and just couldn't accept pity from other people. No, she was going to have to figure out a way to pull herself up by her bootstraps and forge ahead, no matter how difficult.

Laura and Joy consoled her throughout the night until she was delirious from exhaustion. Eventually, she fell into a fitful sleep, worried for the future but too fatigued to remain awake.

The next morning, she awoke and spent the day searching LinkedIn for open jobs. As she'd suspected, she was underqualified for most and the pay was dreadful. Around four o'clock, a knock sounded at her door and she opened it to find a smiling delivery person. He thrust a gorgeous bouquet of flowers in her hands and her eyes narrowed as she contemplated who they could be from.

Setting them on the island in her kitchen, she withdrew the card from the envelope.

Please remember there's always a silver lining, especially for someone as kind as you.

Elated at the thoughtfulness of Laura and Kayla, she made a mental note to give them each super-strong hugs when she saw them at spin class tomorrow. Inhaling the luscious fragrance, she allowed herself to believe, for one moment, that things might just be okay.

J oy chugged the water from her canister, thankful the grueling spin class was over. Smiling at her friends, who sat on the locker room bench beside her, she said, "Thanks so much for the flowers, by the way. They're absolutely gorgeous."

Kayla and Laura exchanged a look. "Not that I want to turn down praise, since I love it," Laura said, flinging her ponytail and batting her eyelashes, "but I didn't send you any flowers, J."

"Me either," Kayla said with a shrug.

"Oh," Joy said as her brow furrowed. "It's this beautiful bouquet of red and white roses. I was sure it was you guys."

"Holy crap," Laura said, eyes growing wide. "You have a mystery admirer. Who could it be?"

Joy racked her brain, thinking of everyone who'd observed her humiliating termination on Friday. "The only person I can think of is Sam," she murmured.

"Oh, the hot IT guy with the huge cock?" Laura asked.

Joy laughed. "I'm not sure if we actually confirmed that, but he is a pretty big guy. I'd peg him at six-four at least. He's not super-muscular, but that's fine. I'd describe him as lean and lanky, but in a good way."

"And you're five-five, so that puts him at almost a foot taller," Kayla said. "Yum."

"He is cute," Joy said, staring down at her hands in her lap. "And so sweet. I'm not sure I've ever met a nicer guy. Too bad I'll never see him again."

"Whoa, who said that? You have his number, right?"

"Actually, yeah. He gave it to me years ago in case I ever needed help with my laptop at home. He mentioned that he does freelance computer repair on the side."

"You have to text him, honey," Laura said. "Tell him thanks for the flowers and take a hammer to your laptop if you have to. It will give him an excuse to come over!"

Joy grinned. "I'll text him, although I'm not going to destroy my computer. He might not have sent the flowers. I still have to figure that out."

"I'm sure he did, Joy," Kayla said. "This is so exciting! You've had such a crap few days, wouldn't it be great if you fell in love with the geeky yet oh-so-sexy IT guy? It's like a cute rom-com."

"Okay, slow down, ladies. I'll text him once I'm home and showered and can re-read the card that accompanied the flowers. I'll let you know!"

Once Joy was home, freshly showered and dressed in her most comfortable sweats, she sat down on the couch and ran the pad of her finger over the white rectangle that held the message.

Please remember there's always a silver lining, especially for someone as kind as you.

Lifting her phone, she composed a text.

Joy: Hi! It's your former co-worker. Wow, that sounds formal. Anyway, I have a super-random question for you.

The text bubble showed up, indicating he was typing back. Joy felt her heartbeat increase slightly.

Sam: Hey, former co-worker but always-friend. Ask away.

Chewing her lower lip with her teeth, her thumbs ticked away at the keypad.

Joy: Did you by any chance send me flowers? If so, they're extremely beautiful and I want to thank you.

Sam: I did. I got your address from the master list that HR keeps on the server. Realizing as I type how creepy that is. I just wanted to make you feel better. What happened to you was really unfair.

Joy was taken by his thoughtfulness.

Joy: It's not creepy. LOL. It's so sweet. I'm obviously distraught and pissed and angry at the world. They brightened my day so much. Thank you, Sam.

Sam: You're welcome. I know you're probably scrambling around with everything going on, but I might have a possible job opportunity. I think I told you I do freelance IT support on the side. It's been steadily growing and I'm considering upscaling. Would love to meet to discuss.

Joy: That's great to hear! I'd be happy to meet with you, but I don't have any IT skills. I'm lucky if I can remember where the power button is on my laptop.

He responded with a LOL emoji.

Sam: I have something different in mind that might be a perfect fit for you. But don't feel pressured. If you want to meet

on Monday or Tuesday after work at Coffee Stop on West 50th & 8th, I'll be happy to discuss.

Joy contemplated. Honestly, she wasn't in a position to turn down any possible opportunity at the moment.

Joy: Let's do it. I'll meet you there tomorrow at six p.m. Sound good?

Sam: Definitely. Excited to see you. Talk then. Have a good day.

Joy sent him a final text, biting her lip as she relaxed into the cushions and contemplated. What was he cooking up and how could she possibly help? Realizing how interested she was to find out—and how excited she was to hang with Sam—her gaze trailed to the flowers on the island counter. Clutching the sweet note to her chest, she let herself enjoy the first moments of true contentment since Friday's disastrous events.

Chapter 6

S am felt more nervous than if he was about to present to the United Nations. Sensing the sweat on his palms, he rubbed them over his black khakis, telling himself to chill. He'd never hung with Joy outside of work and was scared he was going to say or do something completely stupid. Being embedded with terrible shyness usually precluded him from having meaningful relationships with women, but this was different. He felt a sense of inner protectiveness and responsibility for Joy and her current situation and was determined to help her.

She breezed through the entrance and his heart soared into his throat. Lifting his hand, he gave her a wave. Wispy, straw-berry-blond hair trailed past her shoulders and her azure eyes sparkled above her beaming smile. God, she was the prettiest woman he'd ever seen. If he could dream only of her for the rest of his days, it wouldn't be enough.

"Hey," she said, shrugging off her coat and throwing it over the stool. Sitting down, she looked around the coffee shop. "Busy place. You come here a lot?"

"I live a few blocks away," he said. "They have great coffee and strong Wi-Fi, so I come when I need to get out of the house."

"Awesome," she said, waving at the server. The nice lady took their order and Joy rested her chin in her hand, elbow on the table.

"So," she said, her gorgeous smile unwavering. "What's this incredible opportunity? I'm dying to hear."

Sam cleared his throat, reminding himself that this was business. It didn't matter that every muscle in his body was tense with longing for her. No, this was about helping her rectify the terrible wrong that had been forced upon her.

"You know I have this freelance IT business," he said, observing her nod. "It started because my downstairs neighbor would always ask me for help when she saw me checking the mail. Simple things like how to set up her personal email on her iPad, how to wirelessly connect her printer to her desktop, and which malware protection program to install. She has two sons in their thirties who try to help her when they visit, but they're not local and she struggles with the technology. Every time I would help her, she'd insist on giving me fifty dollars. I always refused to take it, but she'd slip it under my door and, eventually, I realized arguing with her was futile."

Joy's expression was wistful, causing him to smile.

"What is it?"

"Nothing," she said, shaking her head. "That's just so sweet. You're a really good guy, Sam."

"It's no big deal, really. I love helping people, especially with tech. It's not as hard as it seems."

"That's what makes it even better. You're just nice to be nice."

The server arrived with their coffees and Sam had to shift on his stool when Joy pursed her lips and blew over the cappuccino. She was wearing some sort of pinkish glossy color that had tiny sparkles in it. Visions of having the sticky substance smeared over his chest from her ardent kisses flashed in his head, and he felt a muscle tick in his jaw.

"Okay, go on," she urged, dragging him from his fantasies.

"Well, Gretchen—that's my neighbor—eventually introduced me to several of her friends, all in their sixties, who needed help. In turn, they connected me with a bunch of their friends. At this point, my entire weekend and most nights after work are consumed with these freelance appointments. I'm starting to pull in decent money and have been toying with leaving RMG to pursue the business full time."

"How exciting!" Joy said, taking a sip of her coffee. It left a small white dab of foam above her upper lip, making her look adorable. Her tongue swiped out to lick it away and he felt his nostrils flare. *Down boy.*

"I've always wanted to start my own business," she said, oblivious to his lascivious thoughts, "but I've never had the capital to do it. My mom has dementia and lives in assisted living on Long Island. It's really expensive and most of my income goes toward covering her bills. And toward living in Manhattan, although I can barely afford it," she said, giving a sheepish grin. "But I love the city. I'll stay here until my landlord drags me out by my hair."

Sam chuckled. "I'm sorry to hear about your mom," he said, feeling a deep well of compassion for her. He'd lost his own parents to a car accident when he was young and had grown up in the foster system in Westchester County. It was lonely and quite isolating. "Is your dad still in the picture?"

She shook her head. "Heart attack over a decade ago. The Widow Maker got him. Such a sad day. I think that's what sent my mom spiraling down, but the doctors say dementia is rarely traceable. Still," she said, shrugging, "I know my mom and it broke her heart. I think it somehow broke her mind as well."

"I'm so sorry, Joy," he said, unable to squelch the need to comfort her. Grasping her hand as it sat atop the table, he squeezed. "That's so hard. I lost my parents when I was five."

"What?" she asked, enfolding his hand in return. "Oh, Sam, I had no idea. I'm so sorry."

"I've had a long time to process it. Car accident in White Plains. I grew up in the foster system in Westchester until I was seventeen and then I enrolled in community college. Got my bachelor's, learned how to program and got my IT certification. I'm luckier than most."

"Do you have any family?" she asked, eyebrows drawn together. "Anyone you spend holidays with?"

"I have a foster sister, Sarah. She's my age and really great. She still lives in Westchester and I see her occasionally. She and her boyfriend invite me over for holiday dinners and I go half the time. Otherwise, I like to stay home and pick up programming jobs. The money is great and I can do it remotely."

Joy's expression was filled with such genuine sympathy that he emitted a small chuckle. "It's fine," he said, clenching her hand once more before letting it go. Otherwise, he was going to start to sweat again and he was pretty sure that sweaty palms were not sexy. Nope, definitely not. "I'm in a good place. I was surrounded by a lot of good therapists and social workers in the foster system and I'm pretty well adjusted. I think," he said, sending a good-natured, contemplative glance toward the ceiling.

Her laughter surrounded him, melodious and lilting. "You seem pretty well adjusted. You're always welcome to hang with me and Corinne during the holidays. I mean it. My sister's awesome and she's a great cook. I'm a solid dish washer, so that's all you get with me."

He laughed. "Noted. Thanks." The kind offer was just another manifestation of her generous spirit. "So, anyway, back to the business. I think I'm ready to leave RMG and start it up, but I'm going to need a business manager."

"Okay," she said, her expression slightly confused.

"Someone who can take calls, communicate with customers, schedule my appointments—in person and online—keep the books and all that jazz. There's no way I can be the full-time tech and do that stuff. I was wondering if you'd like to give it a try."

The shock on her face was evident. Blood coursed through his veins as he waited for her response. Would she think him strange for asking her? After all, he had no proven track record and pledging to work for a startup was a huge risk for someone in her position.

"I..." she seemed to struggle for words. "I'm honored you would think of me, Sam, but taking a chance on a new business would be a really big gamble for me. Plus, I have no experience with bookkeeping. Scheduling the appointments and managing your calendar would be no problem, but I don't want to mislead you on my qualifications."

Straightening his spine and leaning in, he began making his case. "First of all, I completely understand your reservations about the risk. I've thought about that a lot. I have a few provisions in place that I think will make the offer more tenable."

"Okay," she said, nodding.

"Like I said, I've been doing freelance work for years. I keep all that money in a separate account and have invested it wisely. I also like day trading and am pretty good at getting a return."

She bit her lip, the plushy skin squishing underneath her teeth. "I'm starting to think you're a secret genius. How many other skills do you have?"

He breathed a laugh. "Day trading is just math and watching the market. I've always had a knack for it. Same skills used in playing cards, which I love by the way."

"Poker?"

"Yeah," he said, feeling his cheeks warm. At this point, she was going to think he was a degenerate gambler who never left the house. "Among other games. Anyway, my investment account has several hundred thousand dollars in it at this point. I'm going to use that to fund the business."

Her eyes grew so round, he thought they might pop out of her head. "Wow."

"Yeah," he said, the embarrassment now permeating every cell in his body. Sam was always uncomfortable being the subject of any conversation. Wanting to shift back to the matter at hand, he said, "So, that should give you some confidence in the viability of the business, and I'm prepared to pay you the same salary that RMG paid."

Her jaw dropped, mouth forming a perfect "O". "Sam, I worked there for years and figured out how to maximize their raise structure. I was making almost ninety thousand a year. I wouldn't expect you to offer me that, especially since I don't have any bookkeeping experience."

"No one is more organized than you, Joy," he said, remembering all the color-coded spreadsheets she would create so the office had a unified schedule each week. "You could learn QuickBooks, or some similar program, in hours. I'll teach you. I have no doubt you can do it."

"I mean," she slowly shook her head, awe stretched across her attractive features, "I really appreciate your faith in me, but I..." She waved her hand, struggling for words. "I just don't know, Sam. It's a huge risk. For both of us."

"It is," he said, "and I can't guarantee it will be successful. But, I'm a hard worker with an already established and growing client base. That's more than most startups have. And I like the idea of building something from the ground up."

"Me too. As I said, I've always thought about working for myself. Then, I'd never have to deal with assholes like Drake." She scowled and he noticed her fingers clench around the cappuccino.

"What about this? Instead of paying you ninety thousand a year, what if I pay seventy-five and make you part owner? It would give you equity and alleviate any concerns about me overpaying you. In the end, if we're successful, you'll gain more from the equity and you'll have a stake in ensuring the company prospers."

"I can't take part of your company! It's yours."

"Not if we build it together." Sliding his hand over hers, he cupped the soft skin. "I want you to be as invested in building this as I am. We could build it together. You said you've always wanted to be an entrepreneur. Here's your chance."

Her cobalt irises darted between his. After a moment, she asked, "Why are you offering this to me, Sam? I don't understand." Lifting her hand, palm facing out, she said, "I mean, I'm extremely grateful, but have no idea why you're contemplating working with a recently fired executive assistant who isn't even qualified for what you need."

"Your firing was bullshit and we both know it. I overheard Drake saying there were errors in your work. That's impossible. No one is as thorough as you, Joy. He was trying to get rid of you."

She sighed. "He was. The son of a bitch altered the documents. I'm suing him and RMG, by the way. My friend Kayla is a lawyer. She's going to help me."

"Good," Sam said, wondering if he should bring up the screenshot of Drake's email. Deciding it wasn't the time, he carried on. "I hope you fry the bastard. In the meantime, I don't really want to work at a place that employs assholes like him. You'll be doing me a solid if you agree to partner with me and become my business manager, Joy. I can't do it alone. I'd really like your help."

He withdrew his hand, missing the feel of her skin, and sat back on the stool, allowing her to think. She gazed at the floor, thrusting them into silence, as she pondered. Finally, she lifted her gaze to his. After her lips curved into a smile, she asked, "So how much equity are we talking here?"

Sam exhaled, visibly relaxing. Arching a brow, he said, "I was thinking thirty-five, sixty-five."

"No way," she said, incredulous. "That's way too much. I was thinking ten or fifteen percent."

"Don't devalue yourself, Joy. I'm going to need you to work abnormal hours and the effort required is going to be extensive. Since I help people in their homes, I have to work around their schedule."

She gnawed on her lip, the action causing his insides to turn to jelly. "Thirty-five percent, seventy-five thousand a year and health insurance, right?"

"Yep," he said. "I already have an LLC set up and I'll purchase health insurance for both of us through that."

She inhaled a deep breath, blowing it out through puffed cheeks. Latching her gaze to his, she lifted her shoulders. "Holy shit. Let's do it."

"Yeah?" he asked, elation coursing through him.

"Yeah. What the hell? You're offering me a fantastic opportunity. Why the heck are we alive if we're not going to take some risks, right?"

"Right," he said, unable to control his grin. "Holy shit."

Jubilation was evident in her laugh as she threw back her head. Sam observed the pale skin of her neck, aching to touch it with his lips. Returning her gaze to his, she reached over and grabbed his hand. "Let's start a freaking business together. I'm so pumped."

And that was the founding moment of SamJoy IT Services.

Chapter 7

S am put in his two weeks' notice at RMG on Tuesday. During that time, Joy was tasked with several things, including learning the payroll and financial software management programs, as well as setting up social media sites for SamJoy. Sam had updated the website on Monday night to reflect their new company name and Kayla offered to help them incorporate the dba name in the LLC, as well as restructure it so Joy owned thirty-five percent.

"This is amazing, honey," Kayla said on Tuesday afternoon, speaking to Joy from her midtown law firm. "Talk about things working out."

"I know," Joy said, stretching her legs under the wooden desk she used at home. "I honestly can't believe Sam offered this to me. I'm determined to make us the most sought-after IT service firm in Manhattan."

"He sees your worth, Joy. We all do. In the meantime, Kevin is looking over your case. I'll keep you updated with the details."

"Thanks so much," she said, overwhelmed at her support system. She was so damn lucky.

Sam came over on Wednesday so Joy could bring him up to speed on everything. He'd offered to meet her at the coffee shop, but she felt comfortable with him and her desk had become a solid workstation. When the knock sounded at her door, her heart skipped and she couldn't control her smile.

"Hey," she said, head tilted back as he stood before her in the hallway. "You made it."

"I made it," he said, holding up a bottle of champagne. "I figured we should toast to the new business."

"Bubbles are my favorite," she said, pulling back the door and gesturing him inside.

"I thought I noticed you gravitate toward champagne at one of the work happy hours we had. I think it's a good brand."

Joy assessed the bottle and set it on the counter, turning to grab two glasses from the cabinet above the sink. "It is good. Nice choice." She popped the cork, the sound echoing in the room, and poured them two full glasses. Handing one to him, she clinked hers against it. "To our new company. Thank you, Sam. I'm so ready to kill it for you."

"For us," he said, the deep timbre of his voice washing over her. The darker flecks in his light hazel eyes seemed to shine as he grinned down at her, and his lips were full against the rim of the glass. Swallowing thickly, Joy realized how attracted she was to him.

While it was easy to be attracted to someone as viscerally sexy as Drake, Sam was more reserved. More intense. But she realized there in the kitchen, as his large body loomed over hers, he was just as attractive, if not more so. After all, Sam had a sweet charm that most overtly sexual men lacked. Whether it be their ego or their lack of giving a damn, excessively hot guys were usually duds on the personality scale.

But Sam was smart and kind, and those eyes...they seemed to bore into her as his lips curved. "Not to be weird, but I'm going to start to sweat if I don't take off my coat."

"Oh!" she said, setting the glass on the counter and shaking her head. Extending her arms, she watched him shrug out of his jacket. His biceps were toned under his short-sleeve polo shirt, causing her to wonder how she'd ever classified him as lean. Although he was tall, the muscles of his arms were firm and his shoulders were broad.

Taking his coat, she hung it on one of the hooks by the door. Urging him toward her desk, which sat in the corner by the large window, she patted the stool. "I only have one office chair, so you'll have to work with the stool for now."

"No prob," he said, setting his champagne on the desk and settling in. "Show me what you've got."

Scooching forward in the wheeled chair, she pulled up everything she'd been working on for the last two days. After detailing him, she sat back and bit her lip. "So, what do you think? We're all set up on social media and I'm a QuickBooks expert thanks to YouTube. Our business calendar is ready and synced with your phone. I can start marketing and taking appointments if you're ready."

"This is fantastic," he said. "You accomplished so much in two days. I knew you were the perfect person to build this with, Joy. I'm so excited."

"Me too!" Finishing the last of her champagne, she felt her stomach growl. "I'd love more champagne but I think I need to eat something first. Want to order in?"

"I, uh..."

"You must be starving. You came here straight after work. Let's order Italian."

"Okay," he said, giving her a hesitant nod. "But I don't want you to think you have to hang out with me outside of work. I can pick up something on the way home."

"Don't be ridiculous," she said, pulling up the delivery app on her phone. "I'd love to hang with you, as long as you don't mind chilling in my apartment. And, by the way, I think we should make this home base, for now at least. Renting office space is too expensive and coffee shops are too loud for me to schedule appointments over the phone. So, we'll just work out of my apartment until we can afford to rent a space. Sound good?"

Hazel irises darted over her face, contemplating. "I don't want to impose on your space. We could work out of my place too."

"You still have a week and a half at RMG. I think it's easier for us to make this home base."

Sensing his hesitancy, she slid her fingers around his wrist and squeezed. "I trust you, Sam, and feel most comfortable here. Let's not make this complicated."

"Okay," he said, his shoulders seeming to release some of their tension. "But you have to kick me out if I'm driving you crazy."

"Never," she said, lifting her phone to scroll through the app. "Okay, I'm a penne vodka girl all the way. Carb overload for me tonight. What do you want?"

"Gnocchi in bolognese?" he looked to the ceiling, squinting, "or chicken marsala? Always a toss-up."

"This place has the best chicken parm," she said, "if you like that sort of thing."

"Actually," he said, shrugging, "I'm lactose intolerant. So, no parm for me, unfortunately."

"Wait," she said, her features drawing together. "You mean all that time I got you coffee with milk, you never drank it?"

"I..." he rubbed the back of his neck, giving her a sheepish grin. "I always gave it to one of the guys. It was such a nice gesture and I didn't want you to think I wasn't grateful."

"Sam," she said, slightly exasperated, "you should've just told me. Man, I feel like an idiot. I could've gotten you black coffee, you know."

"It's no big deal. Really."

"Okay, knowing this, I'm making an executive decision. This place has amazing chicken marsala, so that's what we're ordering for you." She winked at him, noticing his cheeks flush red. The heat seemed to permeate toward her, surrounding her, and she cleared her throat. Was he attracted to her? He'd always been so polite and platonic, but there was no mistaking his reaction to her.

Interesting.

Getting involved with him romantically would create an entirely new dynamic in their relationship—one she wasn't sure was smart. But she also believed in fate, or kismet, or whatever people called it these days, and hadn't had a boyfriend in so long. What would it be like to kiss Sam? Would he pull her into his firm body and be gentle or dominant? Or, perhaps a combination of both? Suddenly, she was dying to find out. *Uh oh.*

Reminding herself to stay focused, she ordered dinner and poured them another glass of champagne before they sat down to sign all the documents for Kayla, solidifying their business.

S am sat beside Joy on the couch, taken with how enthralled she was by Netflix's newest epic fantasy series. An avid fan himself, he hadn't considered her someone captivated by fantastical stories, but what did he know? Turning her head, her expression was full of excitement.

"Can you believe the mage might actually end up with Henry Cavill? I mean, who saw that coming?" She engulfed a bite of pasta, chewing as she regarded him.

"It's a twist, for sure," he said, finishing the last bite of the succulent chicken marsala. "Can't believe you like this sort of thing."

"Like?" she asked, holding up the remote and muting the TV as the episode faded to black. "I freaking love it. I think I read Lord of the Rings a hundred times when I was in middle school."

Sam chuckled. "Be still my geeky heart."

Joy chewed her bottom lip, spurring him to shift on the couch. Sitting next to her was glorious torture, and seeing her lip squish below her teeth caused blood to shoot to every cell of his dick. Fuck, it was uncomfortable and highly arousing, all at once.

"Are you really that much of a geek?" she asked, one eye squinted as she studied him. "I think you're just a really nice guy who's a bit shy, and who happens to be a whiz at all things tech."

"I am shy," he said, feeling his cheeks warm. He'd always been unable to control his blushing and his sweaty palms, and now just tolerated them as unwanted results of his nervousness. Especially around women. Exponentially around Joy. "It was just hard, growing up with new sets of parents every few years, moving around to new schools. Kids are tough and I found it difficult to fit in. Eventually, I learned to be comfortable on my own. I wish I'd learned to acclimate more, but it wasn't easy for me. Now, I'm just so used to being on my own, I don't really crave the company of other people."

He thought he saw her chin wobble and realized he was painting a completely unflattering picture. Fuck. She was going to think he was some sort of unsociable loner who hated other people. That wasn't the case—instead, he just had a hard time connecting sometimes.

"Sam," she said, placing her plate on the coffee table and doing the same with his. Scooting toward him, she clutched his hands. "I can't imagine how isolating it must've been to grow up without a family. I want you to know that I'm always here for you."

"Sorry," he said, shaking his head, "I realize how stupid that sounded. I'm totally fine, Joy." She gave him a questioning glare. Laughing, he squeezed her hands. "I mean it. But you're awesome to care. That's one of the things that's so great about you. You really care about people. We need more of that in this world."

"Of course, I care," she said. Inching toward him, their knees brushed, causing his shaft to twitch in his pants. "I want to introduce you to my friends. They're super-fun and they'd love you."

He chuckled at the earnestness in her expression. "I'd be some kind of loser if I let you force me on your friends. That's not what I'm after here."

"Stop it," she said, her nostrils flaring. Now her cheeks were red, flushed with frustration at his refusal. "I won't take no for an answer. We're all going out this Saturday. Kayla's boyfriend, Carter, is in a play, and after that, we're heading to a late dinner. You're coming with us."

"Joy…" he said, shaking his head. "I have an appointment with Gretchen on Saturday."

"At six p.m.," she said, arching a brow. "Hi, I schedule your appointments now, remember? It will have to be an hour-long session. I'll call her tomorrow and explain. The show starts at eight, so finishing at seven will give you plenty of time to get to the theater in Midtown."

"This is so sweet, really, but I don't need—"

"It's settled," she said, standing and grabbing the plates before heading over to the sink. Turning on the faucet, she began to rinse them. "Case closed. Moving on." Pivoting, she lifted the bottle. "Want to finish the last of the champagne?"

Unable to control his smile, he stood and sauntered toward her. When only a foot separated them, he stared into her ocean-blue eyes. They swam with sincerity and determination.

"Are you always this stubborn?" he asked, his body thrumming as those teeth sluiced into her curved lower lip. "You might have warned me before I staked my future on partnering with someone so hardheaded."

"Stubborn as an ox, and don't you forget it," she said, beaming. Laying her palm over his heart, he was too overwhelmed by her touch to feel embarrassed at its pounding. "We're in this for the long haul, Sam. We're family now. Get used to it."

He slid his palm over the back of her hand, cupping it to his chest. "Okay. I'll go on Saturday. But if you change your mind, I won't be upset."

"Never," she said, her eyes darting between his. They stood firm, gazes locked, and Sam felt the palpable emotion vibrating between them. Realizing he needed to cut and run before he did something completely inappropriate—like drag her to him and bite that gorgeous lip himself—he lowered his hand and stepped back, breaking their touch.

"I think I'm all champagned out for tonight." The timbre of his voice was low and gravelly. "Text me with updates as you start the social media campaigns tomorrow."

"I will," she said, an underlying wistfulness evident in her heart-shaped face. "And I'll call you when anything else comes up."

Nodding, he grabbed his coat and shrugged it on. "See ya." Turning the knob, he let himself out, hearing the door latch behind him. Once in the lobby, he inhaled a deep breath, leaning against the wall to gather his composure. Joy was offering her friendship, and that was fine. Lovely, in fact. But that was as far as he would ever let it go. Just the thought of having to tell her he was a virgin was extraordinarily embarrassing and humiliating. No, he would never let that happen. Heading out into the cold January night, he shoved his hands in his pockets and trekked home.

Chapter 8

♥

J oy couldn't contain her excitement as she dressed on Saturday. The first week at SamJoy had gone smoothly, and she couldn't wait to update her friends. Moreover, they would get to meet Sam and she was thrilled to introduce them to the man who'd literally swept in and saved her from possible financial ruin.

If she was being honest, she was also looking forward to spending time with him outside of work. After their encounter the other night in the kitchen, she'd barely been able to sleep. Memories of the firm thud of his rapid heartbeat under her palm confirmed what she'd already known deep within: Sam was attracted to her.

Muddying the waters with a random hook-up wouldn't be smart—Joy knew this, of course. But Sam seemed like a relationship kind of guy, not some guy interested in random one-night stands. Smoothing her hands over her dress in front of the full-length mirror in her bedroom, she contemplated how he would react if she suggested they try dating.

He'd seemed skittish the other night, basically bolting from her apartment after their intimate exchange. Was there a reason he chose to remain single? Perhaps a bad experience with an ex? Or, maybe he didn't want to mess with their business relationship? It was a good reason, but Joy felt the sexual energy between them and was a straight-shooter. It would be better to acknowledge it, address it and attempt to find a solution, rather than pretend it didn't exist.

Interestingly, she found herself hoping he was open to dating her. Smiling at herself in the mirror, she began applying eye makeup as the thoughts swirled. Her last relationship with Ted had lasted two years. He was nice, but their spark eventually fizzled and Joy suspected he was losing interest. Sure enough, she'd found the active dating apps on his phone and accused him of cheating. He swore he hadn't slept with anyone else, just gone on a few dates, and that had been the first and last straw. She'd ended it immediately.

After that, dating lost its luster for a while. Joy realized she enjoyed doing things solo and often went to movies and restaurants by herself. Still, she did miss being touched by strong hands, clenching her skin with desire as they drew pleasure from her body. And, man, did Sam have some amazing hands.

Placing her palm on at the base of her neck, she slowly slid it to her breast, gently cupping. It was small but sensitive, and she could almost feel Sam's long, broad fingers toying with her nipple...and the spark of satisfaction as he bit the nub with those amazingly perfect teeth...

Inhaling a deep breath, she dismissed the wetness that was beginning to gather between her thighs. No time for that now, but the thought of being with Sam had implanted itself in her psyche and Joy knew herself. Once she latched onto an idea, she always made it happen. It was probable they would end up in bed together, and she couldn't wait. It had been too long since she'd had sex and she was ready, damnit.

Spritzing perfume at her neck, she heard Sam knocking at the front door. "It's open!" she called.

Giving herself one last glance, a slightly-naughty idea took hold in her mind. Grinning, she reached behind her neck and lowered the zipper, dragging it almost to her waist. Donning her sexy, over-the-knee velvet boots, she stalked into the kitchen.

"Hey," she said, breezing over to where Sam stood by the front door. "Would you do me a favor?" Turning, she pointed to the zipper and stared up into his gorgeous eyes. "I couldn't get it zipped."

His Adam's apple bobbed up and down, causing her to shiver. Oh, yeah, he wanted her big time. Anticipation coursed through her veins. Joy had always enjoyed the thrill of flirting and she was going to take full advantage. Wordlessly, Sam stepped toward her, clutching the tiny zipper in his thick fingers.

A gasp escaped her lips as his skin brushed hers at her lower back.

"Sorry," he murmured, the sound of the zipper so sensual as he slowly slid it up her spine. "My hands are probably cold. I forgot my gloves."

"It's fine," she said, pulling her hair to the side so he could latch the dress at the base of her neck. "Thanks for helping me."

"Sure." His palms gave her shoulders a soft pat, indicating he was done. Rotating, she smiled, loving how far she had to tilt her head to look into his eyes. His height was extremely attractive to her; their size difference making her feel feminine and protected, somehow.

"You look really nice," she said, licking her lips. His hair was still barely wet, light-brown and thick, and the skin of his cheeks was shaved smooth. Would it feel soft against the curve of her breast? Would he grow tiny whiskers if he stayed the night? Boy, she'd love to find out.

Her eyes trailed down his body, assessing his jeans and loafers.

"You said casual but, now that I see you, I think I'm really under-dressed." He unzipped his coat, baring his buttoned-down shirt. "At least I'm wearing a dress shirt." It was tucked nicely into his belt, summoning an image of her fingers unbuckling it as he gazed at her with longing.

"You're perfect," she said. "This dress is really comfortable and so are the boots, surprisingly. The theater is a few blocks from here, so we can walk. Ready?"

"Ready," he said, offering her his arm.

Clutching him close, they headed into the night.

As the crisp winter air flooded Sam's nostrils, he accepted that he would be in a constant state of arousal until at least midnight. Or later, depending on how late they stayed out. Joy looked amazing, her wispy hair curled and full. Her almond-shaped eyes were traced in black, as well as her lashes, and he felt so honored to be the one escorting her down the busy Manhattan street. The aroma of her perfume permeated his senses, cursing him with the desire to bury his nose in her neck and lick it away.

When she'd asked him to zip her dress, he thought his knees might buckle, causing his body to crumple to the floor. That certainly wouldn't have been at all attractive, and he was thankful he'd kept his wits. The skin of her back was so smooth, and when the backs of his fingers brushed it, he'd sent a thousand silent prayers of thanks to the universe. If he only ever touched that part of her, it would be enough. It was certainly more than he'd ever hoped.

As they approached the theater, Joy waved at two women standing by the large front doors. They waved back, both very pretty with bright smiles.

"Hey, ladies," Joy said, her arm still latched with Sam's. "This is my friend, new boss and overall savior, Sam. Sam, this is Kayla and Laura."

"New *partner*," Sam said, shaking both their hands. "I've already realized that Joy is the superstar in our company. I just do the grunt work."

"So nice to meet you, Sam," Kayla said, her brown eyes kind and warm. "Thanks for recognizing how amazing Joy is. We're so excited about your new venture."

"And we're so thrilled she has such a smart, *handsome* partner," Laura said, eyebrow arched over her multi-colored hazel eyes. "This is going to be fun."

Joy gave her a light-hearted glare. "Don't mind Laura. She's on a one-woman mission to size up every single guy in Manhattan. Sam is actually one of the good ones."

"Oh, I bet he is," Laura murmured, waggling her eyebrows.

Sam laughed. "Well, thanks. Working with Joy for the past two years at RMG has been awesome and I think we're going to do some great things together."

Joy shot Laura a glare, cutting off her retort, which Sam sensed would've been slightly suggestive. Feeling his lips curve, he curbed his chuckle.

"Carter got us seats in the front row," Kayla said. "So freaking cool. I guess there are perks to dating the star of the play." She grinned and flicked her hair.

"Great," Joy said. "Let's head in. I'm excited to see him."

They situated in the front row, the seats small and compact. Joy's shoulder rested against his as the lights dimmed, and Sam did his best to focus on the performance. Tough, since her hair smelled absolutely amazing.

The play was a dramatic comedy focused on a family with two young children, a bi-polar father and a mother with depression. Sam found the story compelling and the actors were phenomenal. Glancing over at Kayla, he noticed her smiling with pride as she watched Carter, and he could feel her love emanating toward the stage. It moved something in Sam, who hadn't had much luck in the dating world, mostly due to his shyness and sexual history. Non-history, really.

Self-annoyance surfaced and his gaze drifted to Joy. Out of the corner of his eye, he studied her. How would she react if he told her he was a twenty-nine-year-old virgin? Would she laugh? Feel pity? Think him a total idiot incapable of even talking to women? Sighing, he decided he just didn't have the temerity to find out. No matter how badly he wanted her, he had to keep their relationship platonic. He didn't think he'd survive if she looked at him with anything but the kindness she so often bestowed upon him. No, the current incarnation of their relationship was enough. It had to be.

"Do you like it?" she whispered, face tilted up to his.

Crap. She must've noticed him studying her like a lovelorn sap. "Yes," he whispered back. "Carter's really good."

She nodded, excitement in her ocean blue eyes. God, they were magnificent. Would they sparkle like that as he made love to her? Clearing his throat, he focused on the stage, determined to push the arousing thoughts from his mind.

The curtain fell to raucous applause and a standing ovation. As Carter took his bow, he winked at Kayla and she mouthed I love you to him. Sam found it incredibly touching.

Afterward, they headed to a wine bar near Kayla and Carter's apartment in Hudson Yards.

"This is a nice area," Sam said, shrugging off his coat and sitting at the high-top table. "I live on West Fifty-Fourth but haven't had a chance to explore Hudson Yards much."

"We like it," Kayla said, shooting Carter a smile. "We decided to move in together back in March when my lease was up. Once Carter's lease expired in June, we got a place here. It's much bigger and has an elevator, thank god. No more walk-ups for me, ever."

"And Carter only had a few mild heart attacks at the thought of moving in together, right, Carter?" Laura teased.

"It was the biggest commitment I'd ever made, that was for damn sure," Carter said. "But Kayla promised she would only wear lingerie in the house and give me two neck massages a day, so I capitulated."

Kayla rolled her eyes. "He's such a charmer, no?"

"Don't roll your eyes at me, woman," he said, sliding his arm around her and smacking a wet kiss on her cheek. "You know you love massaging me."

"Shut up and order me a wine," she said, scrunching her features at him.

Reaching for the menu, he took stock of the selection. "Let's see...what will get you most wasted so I can ravish you tonight?"

"Well, I'd like a Malbec before I drown in my own barf," Laura joked. "You guys are so cute it makes me want to gouge my eyes out. Who's sharing with me?"

Malbec was a popular choice, so they ordered a bottle for the table. Carter gave Sam an affable smile. "Really cool to meet you, Sam. I've heard good things from Kayla. Spoiler alert: these three tell each other everything," he said, gesturing between the ladies, "so be careful what you divulge."

Sam chuckled. "Noted, thanks. Great to meet you too. You were fantastic in the play. How long have you been acting?"

"I did commercials for years," he said, sipping the wine the server had poured into his glass. "But about a year ago, I was hit with inspiration to try theater acting again. I guess you could say I met my muse." His arm tightened around Kayla's waist.

"That's awesome," Sam said, lifting his glass in a salute. "To true love."

"Aw, he's a romantic and super-tall," Laura said wistfully, chin rested in her hand as her elbow rested on the table. "Snatch him up, Joy, or I'm gonna do it for you."

Sam chuckled. "Joy and I are strictly business partners. But I'm really excited to build SamJoy with her."

"Well, thank god for some testosterone. I was drowning over here. Sam, I need you to follow bro code and hang out with us as much as possible. Hanging out with three chicks all the time is maddening. I don't think I've used a razor that isn't pink for six months now."

"You're complaining about hanging out with three chicks?" Kayla asked. "What have you done with my boyfriend?"

Carter laughed. "True. What red-blooded male would complain about hanging with you smokin' hot babes? I rescind my statement. But Sam can still hang. He seems cool."

"Thanks, man," Sam said.

Joy beamed beside him, turning his insides to jelly. "Sam's always welcome. I've told him he has no choice but to hang with us when he's free."

"Sweet," Laura said. "So, Carter, you're totally going to be nominated for a Tony. I hope you'll still remember us little people."

"Eh, I'll keep you around, Cunningham," he said, calling her by her last name. "Until I get really famous."

Laura stuck her tongue out at him, and the conversation turned to Carter's career, then Sam and Joy's new company. As they were finishing the last of their second bottle of Malbec and plethora of appetizers, Sam noticed Joy yawning beside him.

"I'll share an Uber home with you if you're ready," he murmured to her.

"Thanks," she said. "Is it that obvious I'm fading?"

After cashing out their portion of the tab, they called the rideshare and said goodbye, heading out into the cold night.

"Burr," Joy said, threading her arm through his and pulling him close. "I'm freezing." It was hard for him not to notice how perfectly she fit into his side.

"James in a blue Camry is only two minutes away," he said, glancing at his screen. He pulled her tight, assuring himself it was just to keep her warm. *Right.* She rested her head into the crook between his arm and shoulder, causing his body to tighten with longing.

Once they were in the car, they chatted on the short ride. Her apartment was first, so she hopped out and waved. "I had a really fun time tonight, Sam. Thanks so much for letting me coerce you to hang with us. I hope you liked everybody."

"They were great. I might let you force me to hang again one day."

Laughing, she nodded. "Night."

"Night," he said, loving how her cheeks were flushed from the cold. It made her look young and sweet, and he ached to hold her.

When he was home and tucked in bed, Sam had no choice but to ease the erection that had plagued him at various times throughout the night. Lowering his hand, he gripped his shaft, working himself as her face flitted through his mind.

"Joy," he whispered, eyes closed as he imagined kissing every inch of her silken skin.

Chapter 9

♥

S am finished up his two weeks at RMG, bidding the place good riddance as he walked out the door on the cold late-January day. Will, Jamal and Frank had given him a bottle of Pappy Van Winkle—which he considered too extravagant but would happily drink anyway—and Sam promised to keep in touch.

Bursting with anticipation of seeing Joy, he almost skipped to her apartment. She pulled open the door, blinding him with her smile as she said, "Congratulations, partner! We're now one hundred percent in this. Hope we don't blow it."

Chuckling, he walked into her embrace, her scent surrounding him. "We're going to kill it."

Drawing back, she nodded, biting her bottom lip. "Hell yes."

His body tensed, forcing him to let her go. A waft of disappointment flashed across her features and he told himself not to read into it. After all, they'd been spending a lot of time together and he felt the spark too. Sam had noticed her sly, flirty smiles over the past few days and he'd convinced himself it was fleeting. Once they settled into a routine, he was sure her attraction would fade and they would establish a safe, boring, platonic friendship. It was how all his other romantic interactions with women had ended up, so why not this one? He couldn't muddy the waters by acting on the sexual energy between them, no matter how much he wanted to. Sam was terrified of her reaction to his lack of sexual history and didn't want to upset the balance they'd created. Better to just let it lie.

"Where did you go?" she asked, dragging him into the kitchen. "I have bubbly ready. Let's toast and get down to business."

They drank champagne as she updated him on her progress that week. Ads were running on social media sites, the payroll had been set up and his calendar was already booked for appointments starting Monday. Impressed with her efficiency, he complimented her work.

"Thanks," she said, settling into the couch. "It's been really fun so far. I hope it stays that way. We're going to be seeing a lot of each other. I hope you don't get tired of me."

"Never," he murmured, taking a sip of champagne.

A knock sounded at the door and she rushed over, taking the brown bag from the delivery guy. "I ordered sushi," she said, setting it on the counter. "Hope you like sushi. I just guessed. I knew you wouldn't stay if I asked you to, so I just made the decision for you."

Chuckling, he walked over to the counter to help her. "Stubborn as usual," he said. "I like everything but crab. Just tell me how much to Venmo you."

"No way, buddy," she said, arranging the various containers. "This is my treat. You saved my damn life, in case you've forgotten. The least I can do is buy you some fairly good sushi." She winked at him, sending his heartbeat into overdrive.

They settled into the stools that surrounded the island, falling into easy conversation. As they ate, Sam picked up on her sexy little traits. The way the juicy flesh of her tongue eased toward the corner of her mouth when she was debating which piece to eat next. How her eyes closed in pleasure when she slowly chewed a morsel she found particular appetizing. Her slim fingers working the chopsticks with ease, spurring him to imagine them working the flesh of his cock. God, he could imagine it so clearly. Those stunning blue eyes gazing into his as she stroked him, increasing the pace, driving him mad. Hoping he didn't choke on his sushi, he carried on, praying she was oblivious to his salacious thoughts.

A s Joy sat with Sam devouring the delicious sushi, she realized something profound: they *fit* together. Never had she felt so comfortable with a man, and for her, that was extremely important. She was someone who didn't want to have to primp and expend tons of energy for a partner. She had a proclivity for sweat pants and not shaving her legs every day—okay, maybe every *few* days—and she wanted a partner who understood that and still loved her anyway.

Observing Sam as they chatted, she recognized he would be that type of boyfriend and lover. He possessed such a sweet soul and she knew, somewhere deep in her bones, he would accept her flaws and quirks. It only made him more attractive, which stirred the arousal she already felt toward him.

Feeling her focus wander, she carried on their conversation, barely listening as she watching his hands. Large and strong, they maneuvered the chopsticks around the various pieces of sushi, almost dwarfing the tiny sticks. When he set them down to eat the edamame, Joy almost elicited a moan. Broad, deft fingers worked the tiny peas out of the green shells, one by one, then lifted them to his tongue. As he ingested the bites, he would lick the salt off the tips of his fingers and thumb, leaving them slightly glistening. What if he used that wetness to slide the digits over her nipple, squeezing it as he blew the moisture away? The image was inexorably hot and Joy felt her cheeks flushing.

"You okay?" he asked, concern lacing his expression.

"Yeah," she said, clearing her throat. "It's hot in here, right? Let me turn down the heat."

After adjusting the thermostat on the wall, she returned to the stool, telling herself to calm down. Although she suspected that

Sam was extremely attracted to her, she sensed him holding back for some reason. Most likely because getting involved romantically would be disastrous if it ended badly due to their work situation. But, if it went well...they could build so much more than just a business together.

"Why don't you have a girlfriend?" she blurted.

He seemed a bit stunned, chopsticks frozen in his hand halfway to his mouth.

Crap. *Way to ease into it, Joy.* Sheesh.

"Sorry," she said, shaking her head. "That was incredibly rude. I just...you're such a nice guy, Sam. I don't understand why someone hasn't snatched you up. I don't think I remember you mentioning dating anyone the entire time we worked at RMG."

His gaze lowered, eyes searching the counter, and she could tell she'd made him uncomfortable. Contrition washed over her and she reached over to encircle his wrist with her fingers. The tiny hairs there tickled her palm and his skin was warm, most likely from his extreme embarrassment at her questioning.

"I'm so sorry," she said, squeezing. "I can tell I've made you uncomfortable. Forget I asked."

Sam cleared his throat. "It's okay," he said, giving her a reassuring grin. "I, uh, well, it's just not that easy for me. I've dated a few girls in the past but it never seemed to work out. In the end, I realized this modern dating world just isn't for me."

"How so?" she asked, genuinely curious about his past experiences.

"I'm shy, Joy," he said, shrugging. "You already know that. It probably isn't as obvious to you, because I feel extremely comfortable with you, but with most girls, I freeze up."

Her lips curved. "I'm so happy you feel comfortable with me. I was just thinking the same about you."

"I do," he said, taking a sip of champagne. "I've dated a few girls in the past. One while I was in community college, but we didn't see each other a lot because she still lived at home and took care of her younger siblings quite often. Eventually, it fizzled out. I dated another woman, Susan, when I moved to the city, but she came from a really close-knit family and hated New York. We were together a few months before she moved back to Georgia. After that, I tried the dating apps but, honestly, they weren't for me. I find it really difficult to reach out and send a message to a girl, especially when I don't even know her. It's just so impersonal."

"I totally agree," Joy said. "I hate those stupid dating apps. When did it become appropriate for a guy to send you a picture of his junk five minutes after making contact? I mean, *ew*. That's just disgusting."

"No pictures of my junk," he murmured, squinting at the ceiling. "Got it."

"Very funny," she said, smiling. "But, seriously, I hear ya. Dating in Manhattan is like the worst reality TV show ever. I hate it."

"How about you?" he asked. "I can't believe you're single. You're a catch, Joy."

Elation swam through her veins at his compliment. "Well, thank you. I've dated some toads, for sure. After the last one, I decided I was going to focus on me. I became okay with doing things solo and hanging with Kayla and Laura. The next time I date someone, I want it to be the real deal. I'm not interested in just dating to pass the time. I'd rather be single."

"That's awesome. I hope you find someone who can make you happy. You deserve it."

I think I already have.

The words wafted through her mind before she could prevent them from forming. Accepting them, she confirmed deep within what she already knew: she wanted Sam and she wanted him badly. Yes, it was a huge risk considering they had just opened a business together. But life was short and guys like Sam didn't cross your path every day. Staring into his crystal-hazel eyes, Joy solidified the decision to seduce her new business partner.

After dinner, she settled into full-on implementation mode. After all, now that she'd made the commitment to seduce him, why wait? Mentally scanning her brain, she realized she'd shaved her legs two days ago. Perfect. The stubble would be barely noticeable. Those broad hands could roam over her thighs and calves to their heart's desire. How exciting.

"Thanks for the champagne," he said, heading toward the door. "I'll text you tomorrow."

"Wait," she said, tossing the paper towel she'd been wiping the counter with. Striding over toward him, she took the coat out of his hand. "You're just going to bail on me? I have the last two episodes of The Witcher queued up and ready to go."

He smiled sheepishly, his cheeks flushing red, making him look adorably handsome. "I actually watched the rest of the season on Thursday night. It was addictive. I couldn't turn it off."

"Wow," she said, her expression filled with mock indignation. "Low blow, partner. How could you leave me hanging like that? I'll only forgive you if you watch them with me again."

He rubbed the back of his neck, looking uncomfortable. "I don't want to impose. It's Friday night."

"What the hell else am I doing? I insist. We can't start off our partnership with you abandoning me mid-season. I won't allow it." She hung his coat up and then dragged him to the couch by his arm. "Sit. Take off your shoes and get comfy. I'm just going to head to the bathroom and I'll be back."

Once in front of the bathroom mirror, she ran a brush through her hair and applied the glittery lip gloss that tasted and smelled so good. Returning to the couch, she sat on the middle cushion, her body brushing his. Turning on the TV, she settled in.

Halfway through the episode, she could tell that Sam was tense. There was a love scene between the two main characters and she noticed him shifting on the couch. She'd turned off the lights, so it was too dim to see if he was aroused, but she'd bet anything that he was.

"You okay?" she asked, staring up at him.

"Yeah," he said, not meeting her gaze. "It's a pretty intense scene."

"Yeah," Snuggling into his side, she shivered. "I'm freezing. Should I turn up the heat?"

"I'm okay, but whatever you want."

"Well, maybe you can just keep me warm. You can put your arm around me, you know. I won't bite."

He slid his arm over her shoulders, pulling her close. Joy rested her head on his shoulder, inhaling the scent of his skin, exposed underneath the two top open buttons of his dress shirt. It smelled like sandalwood and soap, and she imagined running her tongue from the base of his neck to his nipples...and then even lower.

The show continued to play until the credits scrolled at the end of the season finale. Sparing a glance at Sam, she realized he was softly snoring. Long lashes extended from his closed lids as breath escaped his full, slightly open lips. Studying him, Joy realized how exceedingly handsome he was. How had she ever longed for Drake over Sam? What an idiot she was. Lifting her hand, she smoothed it over his cheek, noticing a tiny smattering of stubble just beginning to grow.

He gasped, eyes popping open as he gazed down at her. His eyes were glazed with sleep and he seemed disoriented.

"Joy?" he asked, eyebrows drawn together.

"You fell asleep," she whispered.

"Oh," he said, shifting as he sat up straighter. Removing his arm from her shoulders, he checked his watch. "Damn. It's almost eleven. I should let you get to bed. I'm so sorry I fell asleep."

"It's okay," she said, disappointment rushing through her at his obvious intention to leave. Didn't he realize she was trying to ravish him? Sheesh, men were so oblivious sometimes.

He stood, raking his hand through his thick hair. "Thanks so much for the sushi and champagne. I'll text you tomorrow." Long legs strode to the door and Joy sighed. Rising, she headed over to open the door.

"Bye," she said once he'd entered the hallway. "Thanks for humoring me and watching the show. Well, sort of."

He laughed. "You're welcome. I love hanging with you, Joy. See ya." He gave her a wave and headed toward the elevators.

Joy's brow furrowed as she closed the door. While she brushed her teeth, she couldn't help but wonder: why in the hell was Sam so hellbent on denying his attraction to her? She didn't know, but she was damn sure going to find out...and then, she was going to destroy whatever silly excuse he'd concocted and get those broad hands on every inch of her body.

Chapter 10

♥

T he first week of February was also the first full-time week of SamJoy IT Services. Sam was thrust into an array of appointments with several new clients and really enjoyed the change of pace. Working with Joy was an absolute dream, as she was the most organized person he'd ever met. Snagging her as his business manager would make an exponential difference in his success and he was extremely proud to build something with her.

On the other hand, he recognized they had a bit of a problem brewing. He wasn't sure when he comprehended it, exactly, but somewhere along the way, Sam realized that Joy was intent on hooking up with him. While he was certainly flattered, he was also dead set in his vow to never let them cross that line. Of course, he wanted her badly, but his status as a virgin, as well as their new partnership, were solid reasons to abstain.

But, oh, how incredibly difficult it was. She was adept at roping him into spending time with her, driving his body into a state of constant arousal. She always seemed to have some reason why he needed to visit her apartment in person. Once he was there, she would detail him on the business matters, but always order food and implore him to stay for dinner. Powerless to tell her no, he would, creating the sweetest torture imaginable.

One night, she rested her head in his lap, relaxing on his jean-clad thigh as they streamed a show about the British royal family. Thirty minutes in, she fell asleep on his leg, allowing him the opportunity to brush his fingers over the soft skin of her temple. He realized she had tiny freckles on her cheeks, and the hair he brushed so gently was feather-soft. He could only imagine having it trail over his thigh as she took him into her mouth, her lips swollen with the shiny gloss, gliding over him as he stared into her gorgeous eyes.

She woke and stirred and he promptly left before he blew his load in his pants. Letting her make her apartment home base for their business had been a terrible idea, as he felt comfortable there and his guard slipped too easily.

On Saturday, she talked him into hanging out with her friends again. Sam really liked Kayla and Laura, and he found Carter to be a really cool guy. Carter met them after his play wrapped up for the night, and the two of them sat at a high-top table drinking beer as the three ladies sang terrible karaoke on stage at one of Hell's Kitchen's best dive bars.

"Man, our women have terrible voices," Carter yelled over the eighties tune they were belting.

"Yeah, they're pretty bad," Sam said, giving a mock grimace. "You're a good dude to support them."

Carter smiled. "Kayla's the best thing that ever happened to me, man. I was such a douche before I met her. The least I can do is let her make my eardrums bleed."

Sam chuckled. "Sounds like true love."

"Sure is." Carter gave a nod. "And how about you and Joy? I think she digs you, man."

"Uh..." Sam toyed with the label of his beer bottle, trying to figure out how to explain the strange predicament he found himself in without divulging too many details. "She's a great girl and deserves someone way better than me."

Carter's eyebrows drew together. "How so? You seem really chill, Sam, and Joy says you're a secret prodigy who's way smarter than I'll ever be. You're not a covert serial killer or something, are you? If so, you're *really* good at covering it up."

He breathed a laugh. "It's just not the right time for me to date anyone right now. I'm fully dedicated to building SamJoy and that's all I have time for. I truly wish Joy the best, though. I hope she finds someone worthy of her."

Carter's brown irises swept over Sam's face. "You're a shit liar, man. It's obvious you're halfway in love with her, if not all the damn way. Take it from me. I know that look. I saw it for weeks in the mirror when Kayla dumped me on my ass for being an idiot. Look," he said, leaning his elbow on the table, "I have no idea why you're fighting it. Maybe because you two are business partners and I get that. But, if I've learned anything in the past year, it's how really loving someone can change you, inside and out, for the better. If you truly care about her, give it a chance. Life is short, man. I lost my mom about a year ago and it was devastating. She never recovered after my dad bolted on her, and I always felt it was such a waste. She had a beautiful soul. If you care about Joy, take a chance."

The women finished their song and Carter gave him a nod, indicating he would move on from the semi-awkward conversation. As the ladies approached the table, Sam was taken with their smiles and laughter. They had all accepted him, no questions asked, and he was truly grateful. Joy slipped her arms around him, spurring a jolt of happiness throughout his frame, and smiled up into his eyes.

"How terrible was it? Was it, like, really awful?"

He smiled, wanting so badly to palm her cheek and place a kiss on her glossed lips. "It was perfect. Carter and I loved it."

"Yeah, it was fantastic," Carter teased, rolling his eyes and sipping his beer. "You three are a bunch of Barbra Streisands."

"Shut it, lover," Kayla said, punching his bicep. "You know you love it when I sing."

Carter drew her close, hands on her hips, and rested his lips against hers. "I love it when you moan, baby. Let's go home and practice."

"Gross," Laura said, eyes rolling back in her head. "Can you two cut the PDA for two seconds? Be more like Joy and Sam. At least they wait until they're home."

"Sam is a perfect gentleman," Joy said, lips curved as her blue eyes sparkled.

"Well, thank you," he said, saluting her with his beer. "I try."

"God, I need a man," Laura groaned. "I'm going to get another beer. Maybe I'll meet someone passably attractive at the bar. Who needs one?"

They stayed for another hour, the girls doing one more terrible Whitney Houston rendition, and then Sam walked Joy home. When they approached her lobby, he bid her goodnight.

"You can come in," she said, desire swimming in her eyes. God, how he wanted to, but he dug into his vow to stay strong.

"Not tonight," he said, hating the disappointment that clouded her expression. Hurting her in any way did disastrous things to his heart, and he disliked being the person who denied her. "I've got that appointment with the new client at eight a.m. before she goes to church."

"Right," she said, her tone thoughtful. "Okay, then. Thanks for hanging with us. I hope you can still hear tomorrow."

Sam chuckled. "We'll see." His hand lifted on its own accord, resting on her upper arm and squeezing. "Thank you for introducing me to your friends, Joy. It means a lot and they're great. I..." he struggled to finish the sentence. "You're just really amazing. I'm honored to be your partner."

"Me too," she said softly. As she turned and walked through the sliding glass doors, Sam felt a piece of his heart splinter. Every time they parted, he physically felt it in his bones. As he walked home on the brisk night, he replayed Carter's words in his head. He'd warned Sam not to waste time, as it was so very precious. Could he get over his fear and allow himself to try loving her, as he so desperately wanted to? Unsure if he would ever have the courage, he shuffled home on the darkened streets of Manhattan.

Chapter 11

I t was almost Valentine's Day and Joy had had enough. Enough of Sam denying his obvious attraction to her and enough of the maddening aversion he seemed to have to them taking their relationship to the next level. Speaking with her friends on the Wednesday before the big day, she twirled a strand of hair around her finger as she lay on the couch.

"It's happening, guys," she said, determination in her voice. "I'm cornering him into taking me out on Saturday and that's all there is to it. We're totally going to bang. I'm even shaving my legs and having my eyebrows waxed. He doesn't stand a chance."

"Do you still have a razor?" Laura joked. "I can send one over."

"Ha ha," Joy said. "Although, I honestly think Sam doesn't care about that stuff. I have no idea why he's fighting this so hard. The only thing I can come up with is the business. Like, he doesn't want to complicate things."

"Well, it's already complicated, if you ask me," Kayla said. "He's obviously so into you. He doesn't stand a chance. Get it, girl."

They giggled as Joy bit her lip. "I haven't had sex in so long, guys. Over a year and a half."

"I think my vagina just shriveled up during that sentence," Laura murmured.

"Oh, hush. We can't all have your game, Laura."

"What game? I've completely lost it. I might as well close up shop and adopt fourteen cats. It's over for me."

"Dramatic much?" Kayla asked. "Relax, sweetie. Your guy is out there. He's just getting ready for you."

"He'd better have a huge cock because waiting is really annoying," she muttered.

"Speaking of, we'll need a full report on Sam's assets," Kayla said.

"I hope I can give you a full report," Joy replied. "I'm going to give it the ol' college try. I hope he can't resist me. We'll see."

"Good luck, hon. Oh, and don't forget that we have the deposition next week for your case against RMG and Drake. Three p.m. at my midtown office."

"Thank you so much, Kayla. I can't believe Kevin agreed to do this on contingency. I don't know how to repay you."

"It's nothing, J. I love you. We'll get those bastards."

"Damn straight!" Laura chimed in.

Signing off, Joy hit the red button on her phone. Biting her lip, she called Sam.

"Hey," he said. His breath was a bit labored and Joy could tell he was walking outside. "I just finished up with the new client on East Seventy-Second. Her apartment was insane. I think she's related to a Vanderbilt or something."

"No way," Joy said, settling into the couch as she reveled in his deep voice. "Does she have friends she can recommend us to?"

"Yep. I helped her compose an email while I was there. She sent it to her entire ladies-who-lunch group telling them I was available for any IT needs. Holy shit, Joy. This is huge."

"Ah, the ladies-who-lunch. So regally Manhattan. Can't wait to schedule them in."

"We're doing better than I ever could've imagined." Excitement laced his tone, and she could envision his gorgeous smile as he walked in the brisk air. "I think we could break five or six thousand in gross profit in February. That's more than I ever could've dreamed for our first full month."

Joy calculated the figures in her head, as she was intimately familiar with them from the bookkeeping. "Yep, we'll do at least that much. If we keep it up, we'll be on track for ten thousand a month by summer."

"I'm eventually going to have to hire help," he said. "Otherwise, I won't be able to keep up with all the appointments. My first recruits will be Will, Jamal and Frank. I hope they'll be open to joining us. They're fantastic programmers and developers."

"I hope so too," Joy said, nerves clogging her throat as she inhaled a deep breath. Forging ahead, she said, "I think we need to celebrate this Saturday, just you and me. There's this amazing champagne bar in the West Village and I've been dying to go. Want me to make a reservation for us at seven? We can drink tons of champagne and commemorate our future success before we pass out."

Silence emanated through the phone, causing her to clench her teeth in anticipation.

"Sam?"

"Saturday is Valentine's Day, Joy," he said, slight confusion in his tone. "I figured you'd have a hot date or something."

"Dating is annoying. I'm on a boycott. But I'd love to spend the night celebrating with you. Come on, Sam. You've been working so much. We need to let our hair down. One night won't kill us."

He cleared his throat. "I...I don't want to murk the waters here, Joy. You know I think you're amazing, but we just started a business. That has to be my focus right now."

"I know," she said, emitting a soft sigh. "I just like hanging with you, Sam. I don't want to make you feel uncomfortable. I'm sorry. Maybe it was a bad idea."

She could hear his soft breaths through the phone. As the quiet moment stretched, the pounding of her heart increased exponentially.

"I love spending time with you too," he said, his deep baritone making her shiver. "I just...I don't want to give you unrealistic expectations of...anything."

"No expectations," she said, wondering why there was a latent sadness in his voice. "Just a fun night filled with lots of champagne. How can that go wrong?"

He chuckled. "It does sound pretty awesome."

"So...I'll make the reservation?" She bit her lip, anticipation coursing through her veins.

"Okay," he said, exhaling through the phone. "Seven p.m. I'll call an Uber and pick you up on the way."

"Sweet. Don't feel the need to be too fancy. I'll send you the link so you can check out the place. We'll just be relaxed and cozy. Sound good?"

"Sounds good. In the meantime, did you get that appointment rescheduled tomorrow?"

They slipped back into business conversation for a few minutes until they said goodbye. Bursting with eagerness, Joy threw her phone on the counter and trailed into her bedroom, intent on finding the hottest dress that would knock his socks off on Saturday night.

S am exited the elevator, wondering if his heart had ever raced as quickly as it was now. He hadn't taken a girl out on Valentine's Day in years, and he felt rusty and nervous. As he'd told Joy the night they had sushi, he didn't really date after Susan. The few women he'd taken out had been vapid and annoying, and he'd barely been able to hail a taxi fast enough once the meals had ended. After that, his nights had been consumed with gaming at home, playing cards with his friends or at the coffee shop completing various programming jobs.

Inhaling a deep breath, he knocked on Joy's door. Heels clicked on the hardwood of her kitchen before she swung it open.

"Hey," she said, beaming up at him. She wore a dress that looked like a long sweater, deep purple, that clung to every crevice of her body. Black boots that appeared to be made of some velvety material rose above her knees. An image flashed through his head of biting the tops of the boots and dragging the material down her silky legs as he kissed the exposed flesh. Holy shit. It was going to be a long night.

"I thought you were going to wait downstairs in the Uber," she said. "You didn't have to come up."

His now-damp palm extended the bouquet of red roses toward her. "I couldn't let you go without flowers on Valentine's Day. It just didn't seem right."

The delight in her expression was worth every bit of anxiety he'd felt about spending the evening with her. He wondered if he'd ever seen her smile so broadly.

"Oh, Sam," she said, taking the bouquet and smelling the flowers. "They're lovely. Thank you so much."

"You're welcome," he said softly.

"Come on in while I put them in water and then we'll head to the restaurant, okay?"

Nodding, he stepped in, noting the place smelled fantastic. After placing the flowers in a vase upon the kitchen island, she blew out the scented candle that rested there, her puckered full lips causing him to instantly harden. Yep, it was pretty clear he needed to get ready for a massive all-night erection. At this point, it was standard practice for being in her presence, especially when she looked so goddamned gorgeous.

"Ready?" she asked, handing him her coat.

He helped her shrug into it, allowing himself a small whiff of her hair. It smelled flowery and overall amazing, as usual. When she turned to face him, he noticed every inch of her makeup. It wasn't heavy or caked on. Instead, it was subtle, showcasing her long lashes and the roundness of her cheekbones. Her blue eyes shone and he smiled into them.

"Ready," he said.

They called a rideshare to the restaurant and sat down to enjoy some charcuterie and champagne. Each time she would take a sip from the long glass, he would glance at the smooth skin of her neck, longing to place his lips there and suck the skin between his teeth. Would she moan if he gently bit her as he clutched her soft hair in his hand? God, he wanted to find out so badly.

They ended up finishing two bottles of champagne and Sam could tell Joy was somewhat tipsy. She looked adorable as she gazed at him with slightly glazed eyes, shining from the candle burning atop their table.

"I think I'm ready," she said, emitting a small hiccup. "Crap, I'm drunk."

Chuckling, he signaled to the waiter. "Let me get the check and grab our coats. I think it's time to get you home, Cinderella."

She made some fuss about splitting the bill, which he wouldn't even consider allowing, and once they were set, he pulled up his phone to call a ride.

"Don't put in two stops," she said, clutching his arm as they stood under the cold night sky outside the restaurant. "I have something for you at home that I want to give you. We'll have one more drink at my place before you leave."

Powerless to tell her no, he relented, and they slid into the car. While in the backseat, she cuddled to his side, resting her head at the juncture of his shoulder and chest. Protectiveness swamped him and he drew her close, unable to resist clutching her lithe body. She fit him so perfectly, like a puzzle piece that his body had been searching for but only recently found. Fear closed his throat as he realized he never wanted to let her go. How in the hell was he going to find the will to leave her tonight if she looked at him with those wide eyes and asked him to stay?

He silently practiced the statements in his mind.

Joy, I'm a virgin. I'm so afraid I can't please you. I'm terrified you'll laugh at me or think I'm a freak.

He just couldn't imagine saying the words to her. Sighing softly into her hair, he contemplated as they drove along the Manhattan streets. Eventually, the driver dropped them off and they headed upstairs. As they shrugged off their coats, and Sam settled on one of her kitchen stools, he felt his resolve wavering. Clutching the glass of champagne she'd poured before she scuttled to the bedroom to grab the gift she'd mentioned, Sam swallowed thickly, his body pulsing with equal parts desire and doubt.

Chapter 12

J oy grabbed Sam's gift off her nightstand and then trailed to the bathroom. Once there, she quickly brushed her teeth, plumped her hair and applied lip gloss. If she was going to accomplish **Mission: Seduce Sam**, she needed to be fully armed. Giving her reflection a nod, she straightened her spine and approached Sam as he sat on the stool beside the kitchen island.

"It's not much at all," she said, handing him the small wrapped box. "Just something to say how thankful I am for all you've done for me."

"You didn't have to," he said, his smile reverent. "You're an amazing business manager, Joy. We're equals here."

"I'm glad you think so, although I'm not sure that's true." She pointed to the box when he opened his mouth to argue. "Open it. Please."

His long, broad fingers slid under the paper, slicing it open, and Joy felt a visceral reaction in her abdomen. Just watching his firm fingers maneuver the tiny box sent tingles through her entire body. Wetness rushed to her core and her breath became labored. How deft would those fingers be inside her deepest place, covered in her warmth? How would they feel on her little nub as he looked into her eyes and circled them over and over—

"Wow," he said, interrupting her salacious thoughts. "This is so nice, Joy." He rotated the metal in his hand, reading the inscription on the back. "*For my new partner but always-friend.*"

"I figured you needed a nice business card holder since they came in last week. And I wanted you to have something that memorialized our friendship. You're really important to me, Sam."

His Adam's apple bobbed as he swallowed, those gorgeous hazel eyes searching hers. "You're important to me too. Thank you."

She stepped into his embrace, squeezing him with all her might. Pulling back, she took the box and cardholder from his hands and set it on the counter. Sliding her palms over his pecs, she did her damnedest to speak over the blood pounding in her head, her ears...hell, everywhere through her aroused body.

"Sam," she almost whispered, her voice scratchy. "I think it's time you finally kissed me."

Deep crystal eyes bore into hers as he gently encircled her wrists. "Joy," he said, his voice gravelly. "We can't."

Her eyebrows drew together. "Because of the business? Is that why?"

"I..." he looked down, licking his lips, the sight of his tongue causing her to shiver. "Yes, that's one reason. What if we go down this road and it ends badly? We're partners and it could lead to a shit show. I know you don't want that."

"I don't," she said, shoulders shrugging slightly as she contemplated. "But we're adults, Sam. If we commit to communicating and being honest, I think we have a really good shot at making this work."

Sighing, he gently removed her hands from his chest. Standing, he began pacing across the hardwood floor. "It's not just that. There are other...things...I just...I'm not good at this."

"Good at what?" Confusion caused her brow to furrow. "At being in a relationship? I'm no expert either, but couldn't we at least try?"

He shook his head, resting it on his fingers. "It's not that. Fuck, this is so hard."

Concern coursed through her frame. "Do you, like, have some disease or something? You're starting to scare me," she said, only half-joking.

He breathed a laugh. "No." Rubbing his fingers over his eyes, he groaned. "I'm terrified to tell you, Joy. I'm just so afraid you're going to laugh or think I'm a loser."

"Sam," she said, closing the distance between them and grasping his upper arm, forcing him to stare into her eyes. "I won't laugh at you. Whatever it is, just tell me. I promise I'll listen with an open mind."

His irises darted between hers and he exhaled a deep breath. Sliding his hand in hers, he tugged her back toward the stool and sat, positioning her in front of his long legs. Releasing her hand, he said, "I feel so ridiculous."

Smiling, she shook her head, giving him space so he could speak. "Don't. I'm ready. Hit me with it. Are you the son of the Un-abomber or something?"

A laugh escaped his lips, causing them to curve, and she told herself to calm down. This was Sam. Sweet, thoughtful Sam. Whatever he told her couldn't be *that* bad, could it?

"The thing is," he said, awkwardly rubbing the back of his neck, "I've never done this before."

Her brows drew together. "Dated?"

"Had sex," he said, his expression pensive as his gaze drilled into hers.

Joy stared back, blinking as she processed his statement. "You've never had sex before?"

"No," he said, palming his face and swiping it with his hand before cupping his chin. "I'm a virgin, Joy. It's extremely embarrassing and I didn't want to tell you because I thought you'd think I was a freak."

She stood before him, stunned, allowing the information to wash over her while he waited, chin resting in his hand, looking as if he expected her to kick him out any minute. Compassion washed over her and she slowly stepped forward, closing the distance between them.

"That's it?" she asked, encircling his wrist and drawing his hand away from his face. Releasing him, she slid her palms over his cheeks, warm with embarrassment. "You're a virgin? That's all? I thought you were going to tell me you had five bodies buried in your apartment or had seven types of STDs."

He laughed, shaking his head in her hands. "I'm sorry. I didn't mean to scare the crap out of you. I was just so ashamed to tell you. I mean, who in the hell is a twenty-nine-year-old virgin in this world? It's humiliating."

"No, it's not," she said, breathing a sigh of relief. "It just means you haven't had the right opportunity to get your groove on yet. It's better than banging every woman in sight and never calling again. Believe me, guys who do that are jerks. Except Carter. We give him a pass because he totally reformed for Kayla."

Sam's full lips curled into a grin, causing Joy to lick her own in anticipation. For some reason, knowing he'd never been with anyone sexually was incredibly arousing. She could be the first woman he truly let go with; the first one he experienced something terribly important and significant with. Realizing how much she wanted that, she ran the pad of her thumb over his lower jaw.

"I still want you, Sam," she said, dying to feel those thick lips against hers. "If you want me."

His hands slid over her hips, clutching her, causing her body to shudder. God, those broad hands almost completely encircled her waist. She wanted them pulling her naked body into his *now*.

"I've never wanted anything more than I want you, Joy," he rasped. "But I'm terrified I won't be able to please you. I'm really inexperienced at this. I'll die if you're not satisfied. Seriously, I'll dig my own damn grave. I don't want to set us up for that."

"Of course, I'll be satisfied. I'm insanely attracted to you, Sam. Don't you know that?"

His hands tightened on her hips. "I've become aware you might be trying to hook up with me over the past few days. It's pretty much driven me insane."

"And now I realize why you were holding back. Holy crap. You should've told me this weeks ago. We could've had so much sex by now."

His warm chuckle enveloped her. "I just didn't know how to bring it up. I feel like an idiot."

"Well, since we're being adults here, let's get a few things out of the way." He nodded. "First, I have no idea where you got the notion that sex between us will be anything but fantastic. I've had enough fantasies about your hands, alone, to last several lifetimes."

"My hands?" he asked, eyebrows drawing together.

"Oh, yes," she said, biting her lip. "We're going to put those to good use." Noting his sexy grin, she continued. "Second, having sex with someone new is always a bit awkward, but we just need to make sure we communicate. I'll tell you what feels good and you have to do the same. If we do that, I'm pretty sure it's going to be amazing."

"I can do that," he said, pulling her slightly further into his body, his legs parting so she could ease toward him.

"And last, we just need to decide how we're going to handle the safety issue. I'm on the pill and haven't had sex in almost two years. My last checkup was free and clear, but it's up to you if we use a condom. I'm fine with whatever you choose."

His gaze darted over her face as he contemplated. "I trust you, Joy, and really want to connect with you. So, I'm fine not wearing a condom if you're on the pill and if you're sure you're okay with that."

"I'm one hundred percent okay with that," she said, unable to control her smile. God, she must be beaming. Not giving a shit, she let the happiness wash over her.

"I can't believe this is going to happen," he murmured, nuzzling his cheek into her hand.

"Oh, believe it, mister," she said, inching closer until her lips brushed his. "We're going to rock each other's world. Now be a good partner and take me to bed."

Sam growled—a legit, panty-ripping growl—causing her to gush in her thong. She whimpered with delight when he slid those wide palms over her ass, cupping both cheeks. Drawing her close, he sucked her bottom lip between his teeth, gently biting.

"I've wanted to bite that sweet lip since the first day I met you," he murmured, the words slightly garbled as he spoke around the flesh.

"Oh, god," she whispered, sliding her arms around his neck. "Kiss me, Sam."

Gliding one arm up her back, he fisted it in her hair. Eliciting a deep groan, he tilted her head back, parted her lips with his and devoured her.

S am was pretty sure he was dead. How else could he be experiencing the greatest dream he'd ever had? Joy was mewling below him, the soft sounds causing his dick to twitch with longing as his tongue roamed her mouth. She must've brushed her teeth when she snuck to the bathroom because she tasted like mint and sweetness and spring, all rolled into one. Her tongue slid over his, jabbing until he licked her and sucked the tip between his lips. Her body seemed to melt in his hands and he held her tight, not wanting her to fall.

"Good grief, my knees just literally buckled," she breathed into his mouth. "Take me to bed and fuck me."

The words were so erotic, they sent a shaft of desire through his tall frame. "I want you so much."

"Don't hold back," she said, tightening her fingers in his hair, driving him wild. "I want you out of control. No thinking, okay?"

In response, he shot from the stool, lifting her with one hand as the other still gripped her hair. Instinctively, she wrapped her legs around his waist and he carried her toward the bedroom. Once there, he observed the queen bed and the lamp by the dresser that emitted a soft light. Lowering her to the forest green comforter, he stretched over her, nuzzling her nose with his.

"I want to see you," he whispered, reaching for the hem of her dress. "Can I take this off?"

"Yes," she said, lifting her butt off the bed so he could slide the fabric over her hips. Raising her arms, she watched him through hooded lids as he slid the dress off her body. Tossing the garment to the floor, Sam sucked in a breath as he placed his palm on her collarbone. Leaning on his forearm at her side, he slowly slid his palm over the center of her chest, between her bra-clad breasts, and down to her stomach. The muscles there quivered, causing his shaft to reach for her, dying to be inside her sweet warmth.

"Sam," she said, shaking her head on the comforter. "Please touch me." Reaching down, she unclasped the strapless bra, dragging it from her body and throwing it to the floor. Her pert breasts were small with berry-ripe nipples, begging to be touched.

"You're so fucking gorgeous, Joy," he said, hating that his hand trembled as he reached for her breast. Ever so gently, he cupped it in his palm. The ivory globe looked so small in his hand, the tiny nub begging to be toyed with. Gliding the pad of his thumb over her skin, he slid it over her nipple.

"Oh, god," she moaned, head tossed back on the bed. "Please, Sam. They're so sensitive. I like having them tugged and bitten and whatever else you want to do. Just be gentle. *Please.*"

Her ragged cry snapped something within and he closed his fingers around the tight bud. Pinching it, he reveled in how her body bowed beneath him. Unable to resist, he lowered his mouth to the nub and sucked it between his lips.

"Fuck," she cried, pushing her breast into his mouth, offering him the succulent peak as he tried to control the vicious shakes of his body. Tasting her like this was sweeter than the finest wine and he did his best to follow her direction. After swiping her with his broad tongue, lathering the bud with wetness, he gently bit the tip, noticing how she slid her hand down her body and under her cute, violet lace underwear.

"My clit is freaking throbbing," she said, cupping her mound. Gliding his hand down, he encircled her wrist and pulled it to lay limp on the bed. Locking his gaze with hers, he said, "Let me suck your pretty nipples while I touch you here." He palmed her mound, realizing it was slick and smooth. "You're so soft here."

"I wax everything off. Hate dealing with the hair," she said, giving him an adorable smile. "Hope you're not a bush guy because it's probably never going to grow all the way back."

Chuckling, he pressed a soft kiss between her breasts. "I do love a good muff, but I'll survive."

"Is that a joke? I hope that's a joke."

"It's a joke," he said, sliding his index finger between her wet folds. "It's so fucking sexy. You're so slick here." His finger dragged back and forth, and he rejoiced at her resulting squirms beneath him. "Are you sensitive here too?"

"Yes," she said, blue eyes sparkling as she bit her full lip. God, she was the sexiest thing he'd ever seen. "I don't come from penetration, so I need my clit stimulated. Hope you're okay with that."

"I'm so fucking okay with that." Lathering his finger with her juicy wetness, he slid it higher, searching. Finding what felt like a tiny nub, he began to circle. "Here?" he asked, praying he would be able to please her.

"There," she said, her mouth open, lips swollen and wet. "Right fucking there." She opened her legs wider, giving him a magnificent display. His wrist gyrated as he circled her clit, those hot velvet boots still covering her exquisite legs. Lowering his head, he took her other nipple into his mouth, unable to control his groan as he tasted her.

"Ohmygod, Sam," she breathed, the words jumbled together as she writhed below him. "I'm going to come so fast. Don't stop."

He worked his tongue over her nipple, barely able to catch his breath as her soft cries wafted over him. Her hands reached down, pulling the swollen folds apart at her center, opening her further.

Taking her cue, Sam slid his finger back to her center, gathering more of her slick juices, before gliding them back up to her clit. Pressing two fingers to the engorged bud, he circled it with firm, arduous strokes.

"It feels so good..." she moaned, head thrown back. "I'm so close...yes..."

Concentrating with all his might, he pulled her nipple deep into his mouth, sucking it with firm tugs of his jaw. The skin across her collarbone was flushed red, her flowing hair spread across the comforter. Popping her nipple from his lips, he flicked it with the tip of his tongue before closing his teeth around it. Working his fingers with intense focus at her clit, he bit her nipple as her back arched.

She called his name, her body exploding into violent shudders as her legs snapped closed around his wrist. Palming the luscious folds of her pussy, he gently licked her straining nipple. She clenched her hand in his hair as she quaked, indicating it was too much, and he lifted his head, content to just watch her experience the climax.

Head thrown back, body trembling, naked under his clothed body, Sam thanked every god in heaven for the beautiful gift of his magnificent Joy. Laughter escaped her kiss-swollen lips as she slowly recovered from the intense orgasm. Her body fell limp on the bed and she emitted a loud sigh.

"Holy shit," she breathed, eyes closed as her lips curved with contentment. "That was amazing." Lifting her lids, he noticed her eyebrows draw together. "Crap, I'm pulling your hair out. Sorry." Her fingers relaxed in his hair. "I love having everything stimulated but once I start coming, I can't take anymore. Hope you don't have a bald spot."

His free hand gently brushed the hair off her forehead, the other one still cupping her mound. "I'd sacrifice every hair on my damn head to see you come like that every minute of every day. How long until I can do it again?"

She giggled, causing his heart to melt. "Soon. But first, I think it's time I make you come. I want you inside me, Sam. I want to make love to you."

Every cell in his body shattered at the genuine words. Lowering his lips, he consumed hers in a blazing kiss. Lifting his head, he stared at her, overcome with emotion. Telling himself to chill, he inhaled a deep breath. Breaking down in tears definitely wasn't sexy. Um, yeah, not in the slightest. Although being here with Joy, after all the years he'd pined for her, was enough to make him well up like a teenager in the front row at a boy band concert. *Be cool, Davidson.*

She shifted under him and he watched her slide off the bed, languid and unhurried. Resting his head in his hand, his elbow on the mattress, he observed her movements. Placing one booted leg on the bed, she rolled the boot off, slow and sexy. Her gaze never left his, and her smile was mischievous, indicating she knew exactly what she was doing to him.

"Are you trying to make me come in my pants?" he asked, eyebrow arched. "Because I'd much rather be inside you when that happens."

Plopping the boot on the floor, she reached toward him, dragging him to stand. "Oh, I'd much rather that too. Take off your shirt, big boy. We're just getting started."

His fingers almost tore the buttons off his shirt as he struggled to undo them while she ripped his belt free of the buckle. Tossing the shirt to the floor, he shrugged out of his pants and boxer briefs, kicking them free once he'd also toed his shoes off. Standing naked before her, he let her slide her palms over his shoulders and push him to sit on the side of the bed.

"You still have a boot on," he said, his voice low and raspy.

"Oh, I know," she said, waggling her eyebrows. Clutching onto the top of his shoulder, she lifted her boot-clad leg to the bed, opening her still-slick core to his view.

"Holy shit," he breathed, aching to take her breast into his mouth as it sat in his direct line of vision.

With her free hand, she rolled the boot over her knee, slowly dragging it off until it fell to the floor. Stepping back, she hooked her fingers into the purple thong that draped across her hips. Eyes cemented to his, she slid the thong down her creamy thighs, stepping out of them. Closing the distance between them, she rested one hand on his shoulder while reaching down with the other to enclose his shaft in her palm.

Sam hissed a breath, his eyes almost crossing at the erotic image of Joy's small hand palming his cock.

"I have to admit, I thought you'd be big since you're really freaking tall, but you're huge, Sam. I'm a bit intimidated."

"Don't be," he said, his voice cracking like a high school senior about to ask out his first girlfriend. "Remember that I'm the one who has no idea what they're doing here."

Her tongue darted over her lips as she smiled. "I don't think so, buddy. You're a pro. But I do need you to get me wet again."

Gliding his hands over her hips, he drew her to him, unable to resist her succulent breast. Closing his mouth over her nipple, he reveled in the fingers she curled into his hair.

"Let me lay down," she said, popping from his mouth and crawling over him. Lying back on the pillows, she stretched her arms out. "Come here."

Sam fell into her arms, disbelief that this was actually happening coursing through his veins. As he loomed over her, he couldn't help but steal a kiss from her glossy lips.

"Your lip gloss drives me fucking nuts," he whispered into her mouth as he lavished her. "All I ever think about is having it smeared over every inch of my body."

"Mmmm..." she murmured, sliding her tongue over his as her arms encircled his neck. "We'll have to make that happen. I'm very dedicated when I set my mind to something. Have you thought about having it smeared everywhere?" she asked, her tone playful and teasing as she glided her hand down his body to grasp his cock.

Sam nudged himself into her palm. "Every-fucking-where, Joy. Oh, god. Even there."

"Good," she said against his lips. "We'll add that to the list."

"There's a list?" he asked, running the pads of his fingers across the quivering skin of her belly and abdomen before settling them between her swollen folds.

She groaned. "Yes, there's a list. It's in my head but I can write it down." Sam inserted the tip of his finger into her tight channel. "Ohhh, later. I'll write it down later."

Chuckling, he stared into her eyes as he pushed his finger further. "Okay?" he asked softly.

"So okay," she said, the tips of her nails scraping his scalp, driving him wild. "You can do two if you want. I think you need to stretch me. It's going to be tight."

Sam almost lost it, the thought of pushing himself between her constricted folds almost too much to bear. Inserting another finger, he worked them back and forth deep in her core, feeling her relax and open as he played with her.

"I'm ready," she whispered, spearing those sexy-as-fuck nails into the back of his neck. "Please, Sam. Fuck me."

An intense feeling spread over him as he realized he was finally going to shed the secret that held so much embarrassment and discontent deep in his soul. The fact that he was going to finally lose his virginity with Joy, whom he was pretty sure was the love of his life, was almost unimaginable.

"I know," she whispered, palming his cheek. "It's okay."

He slid his body over hers, aligning them. Pushing his leg between hers, he gently urged her thighs apart. The head of his cock probed her center, connecting with her juicy wetness as he moaned.

"Should I rub your clit while I move inside you?"

"We'll get to that eventually. It's okay if you focus on your pleasure too, Sam." Widening her legs, he fell deeper into her body, the head of his shaft encompassed by her slick folds. "Next time, we'll focus on coming together. This time, I just want you to feel."

"I want to please you," he said, placing a soft kiss on her lips.

"You do," she whispered into his mouth. "So much. I need you inside me."

Licking his lips, he gazed deep into her ocean-blue eyes. Feeling more connected with her than anyone he'd ever known, he began to inch inside her sweet warmth. The walls of her core choked him, wrenching the air from his lungs as every cell in his cock exploded with pleasure.

"Joy," he whispered, cupping the back of her head, her soft hair tickling his palm.

"I know," she said again, her nails digging into his back. "I feel it too."

Inch by glorious inch, he pushed inside her, the walls of her pussy swallowing him as if she were made for him. Groaning, he felt the head of his cock nudge against something unyielding.

"You're in all the way," she said, her expression open and trusting. "You can start moving." Her smile was breathtaking as she lay below him.

Focused on her stunning eyes, he began jutting his hips back and forth, unable to control the small groans that escaped his throat. Her taut pussy was like a vise, clenching him so forcefully he thought he might melt into her. The slickness only added to the maddening friction and he closed his eyes, already feeling the orgasm looming at the base of his cock.

"Damnit," he said, teeth clenched. "I'm so close. Fuck. I was afraid of this."

"Hey," she said, lowering one hand to clench his ass, further increasing his pleasure. "It's okay. We're going to do this multiple times tonight. Come if you're ready. You feel so good, Sam. Let go. Fuck me hard if you want to. I can take it."

"Joy," he gritted, the pace of his hips increasing.

"Fuck me," she commanded. "Now."

Growling with pleasure, Sam lifted to his knees, grasping her hips in his broad hands. Loving how her curves flared beneath his fingers, he gripped hard, dragging her body into his. Back and forth, he slammed into her, their bodies joining, the slapping sounds of slick flesh reverberating off the walls. Sam grunted as he watched his shaft impale her, claiming her, marking her as his. Her back arched as he pummeled her, and he felt a tingling sensation in his balls.

"Fuck!" he groaned, eyes focusing on her perky breasts as they jostled back and forth due to his intense pounding. "I'm coming. Oh, god."

She mewled, head tossing back and forth on the pillow.

He screamed her name, feeling his release begin to shoot down his shaft. Spurting into her, he lost all semblance of control. Feeling his muscles turn to jelly, he collapsed over her, panting as his hips jerked, bursting jet after jet of come into her tight channel. Her arms surrounded him, pulling him close as he capitulated to the intense pleasure.

Sam's hips quaked, overcome with sensation. Lost in her tight warmth, he didn't even try to control the trembling of his sated frame. Sliding his arms under her back, he squeezed her against his sweaty skin, wishing she could understand how much it meant to him that she was his first lover.

Joy sighed below him, the sound content and satisfied. Her fingers trailed over his back as he breathed in her scent. Face buried in her neck, he felt the slight twinge of embarrassment flush over his skin, hating he'd orgasmed so quickly.

"You alive there?" she teased, tapping his back.

"Yeah," he groaned, trailing soft kisses along the skin of her neck. "God, Joy, that was intense."

"Mmm-hmm..." she said, sliding her leg over the tiny hairs of his. "So good," she mumbled.

Lifting his head, he gazed into her heavy-lidded eyes. Stroking the hair from her forehead, he gave her a sheepish grin. "It was so fast. I'm sorry. And I need to figure out how to make you come while I'm inside you."

Her resulting smile was the most beautiful image he'd ever beheld. Tracing his lips with her finger, she shook her head on the pillow. "That was amazing, Sam. Sex isn't always about getting off. It's about connecting. I mean, it is for me at least." She shrugged. "I felt so connected to you and I'm so honored to be your first lover."

His sated cock pulsed inside her at the sincere words. "Me too," he said, unable to form a coherent sentence. Somewhere down the line, he'd tell her that she was the woman of his dreams, and if he had it his way, she'd be his *only* lover. Forever. But, for now, he was content just to hold her and let his gaze wander over her exquisite, heart-shaped face.

"How appropriate is it that you lost your V-card on Valentine's Day?" Grinning, she waggled her eyebrows.

Sam laughed. "Pretty appropriate, I guess. Although, I should've done more to earn you. I should've planned something really special for you tonight."

Sighing, she cupped his cheek. "You're so fucking perfect. Do you know that? I'm sorry it took me so long to notice it. I was a complete idiot."

Leaning his head on his hand as his elbow dug into the pillow, he smiled. "Yeah, I was sure you were in love with Drake."

She rolled her eyes. "What a dick. I was infatuated with his looks, which is really stupid. Now I realize you're, like, a thousand times hotter than he is."

"Yeah?"

"Yeah," she said, nodding. "I hope you'll forgive me."

Sam pushed his hips into hers. "I forgive you," he said, nuzzling her nose with his. "You could do just about anything right now and I'd forgive you."

Chuckling, she lifted her lips to his and gave him a tender kiss. "I want you to hold me. Let's clean up and then we can cuddle, okay? Does that freak you out? That I want to snuggle with you?"

"No way," he said, pecking her back. "We'll cuddle and then we'll go again. I promise I'll last longer next time."

A sexy blush rushed across her cheeks. "Well, hot damn."

Pulling himself from her luscious warmth was torture, and his sensitized shaft felt every inch of the loss as he disengaged from her. Rising beside the bed, he extended his hand to her. She grabbed a robe from the hook on the bedroom door and shrugged it on. After she finished in the bathroom, he trailed behind her, washing the evidence of their loving from his cock, anticipating the next time he would be inside her.

Once back in her room, he slid in beside her and pulled her close. She cozied up to his chest, resting her cheek on his pec as her palm settled over his chest. Strumming his fingers through her hair, he reveled in her strong, calm breathing.

"I want to chat but I'm so tired," she said, the sentence finishing in a yawn.

"Let's sleep a bit if that's okay with you. I'm beat too. We did have a lot of champagne."

Giggling, she nodded against his chest. "I was drunk before but, once I realized I needed my wits to seduce you, I sobered up."

"Your master plan worked," he teased, his body tightening as the silky skin of her leg slid over his, entwining them together.

"Thank goodness," she mumbled against his chest.

As she fell to sleep, wrapped in his arms, Sam was taken with the magnitude of the moment. Finally, after twenty-nine long years on the planet, he'd lost his virginity to the woman he loved deep in his soul. For someone who'd had his fair share of unlucky breaks, it was a poignant moment of peace. Sighing with true contentment, he fought off sleep as long as he could, wanting to cherish every second of having Joy in his arms. Eventually, he lost the battle and succumbed to the darkness.

Chapter 13

J oy's hand trailed over Sam's chest, the small, brown hairs tickling her palm. Settling her head on her hand as her elbow rested on the pillow, she studied him. His mouth was slightly open as he snored, his lips set in a slight grin. Was he dreaming of her? She hoped so.

Losing one's virginity after so long was significant. Joy vowed to be worthy of his trust and affection. Sam was an incredibly good man, and she'd known her share of frogs. Building a relationship alongside a business would have challenges, but she was sure they could navigate the process together as long as they remained open and honest.

Sam stirred under her hand, his lids opening as his stunning eyes tried to focus on her face.

"Hey," he whispered, lifting his hand to sift his fingers through her hair.

"Hey," she said, running her palm over his nipple and reveling in his resulting shiver.

"Did you sleep?"

She nodded.

"Were you watching me sleep?"

Chuckling, she bit her lip. "I just don't understand how someone as incredibly attractive and thoughtful as you kept their V-card for so long."

A slight blush covered his cheeks and Joy realized how cute it was that he blushed so freely. He probably hated it, but she found it insatiably charming.

Inhaling a deep breath, he grasped her hand on his chest and lifted it to his mouth, giving her palm a tender kiss. Lying her hand flat over his heart, he covered it with his. Joy felt his strong heartbeat, pumping in time with her own.

"Well, I told you about Christy and Susan. Those were my only two girlfriends, although I'm not sure either relationship was quite that serious. Christy was the one I dated in college. She was a geek too and loved video games. We always hung out at her house because she took care of her five younger siblings while her single mother worked three jobs. We made out some, but I just didn't feel comfortable hooking up with her in her bedroom with five kids outside. You know?"

Joy breathed a laugh. "Not an ideal scenario for sexy times."

"Exactly," he said, grinning. "And Susan came from a religious family and wanted to wait until marriage. That was totally fine with me, but when she moved back to Georgia, I knew it was over. We liked each other, but we weren't the ones for each other. We fooled around during our relationship but obviously never had sex."

"That makes sense," Joy said.

"After that...I don't know." He shook his head upon the pillow. "I tried the dating apps but they were awful. It felt like a cattle drive or something. Every girl I went out with was looking to get married or vying for a free meal, and I was this shy guy just trying to find a nice girl to hang out with. Eventually, I gave up. Then, I met you." His gaze locked with hers. "After that, I didn't really have the desire to date at all."

Extreme tenderness welled in her heart. "Why didn't you tell me you had a crush on me? You should've asked me out."

"I was terrified you'd say no but more terrified you'd say yes, and we'd have a great time and I'd eventually have to tell you I was a virgin. I was just so embarrassed and figured it was easier to let you find someone more experienced."

"Did you really think it was that big of a deal?" she asked. "I think it's so sweet. It shows that being intimate with someone means something to you. It does to me too, Sam. I can count the number of guys I've slept with on one hand. I'd rather be alone than have meaningless sex."

"I should've had more faith in you." He cupped her jaw, rubbing the pad of his thumb over her bottom lip.

"You should have," she said, giving his thumb a soft peck. "I'm honored to be your first, Sam. And, by the way, you're really good at sex. We're going to need to do it a lot."

His deep chuckle surrounded her, enveloping her in its warmth. "I want so badly to make it good for you, Joy."

She shifted, slithering over him, aligning her body atop his. "It's so good," she murmured, cementing her lips to his. "Let's do it again."

His strong arms slid down her sides, his palms cupping the globes of her ass. She moaned when he squeezed them in his broad hands.

"Only if you come first."

She positioned her folds over his thick cock, engorged and ready. "Move me over your cock," she breathed into his mouth. "Rub my clit over it and I'm pretty sure I'll come."

Growling, he began directing her hips, undulating them with his strong hands, propelling her up and down his shaft. Wet juices flowed from her core and they began to spread over his straining flesh, expediting the deft movements. Joy speared her tongue into his mouth, kissing him with all the ardor she felt at finally being in his arms.

As he slid her over his muscular frame, she felt cherished...loved, even. Sam's feelings for her were evident, and she pledged to treat them with care. If they handled this properly, she could see herself ending up with Sam. Forever. The thought brought her such happiness that she felt it to the depths of her soul.

Her clit throbbed as she writhed over him, causing her to moan. Palming Sam's cheeks, she stared deep into his eyes.

"You feel so good against me."

He whispered her name, love shining in his eyes.

Positioning her wet opening over his shaft, she began to slide over him, enveloping him in her warmth.

"Did you...?" he asked, concern in his gaze.

"Shhh..." she said, sliding her hand between their bodies and finding her clit. Circling it, she gyrated her hips above his. "Harder," she commanded.

A muscle twitched in his clenched jaw as he began jutting into her, eyes cemented to hers. His grip was almost bruising on her ass as he controlled the movement of her hips. It was intoxicating...raw...visceral. She felt *claimed* by him. Marked somehow.

"Tell me you like my pussy around your cock," she said, needing the dirty talk to push her over the edge. Joy always imagined her fantasy lovers speaking dirty words when she brought herself to orgasm, and couldn't resist hearing them from Sam's deep baritone.

He groaned, his gaze questioning as he pistoned inside her.

"Tell me," she moaned.

"Your pussy is so tight," he gritted, one hand moving to clutch the hair at the base of her neck as the other retained the grip on her ass. "You're so fucking gorgeous, Joy. I love fucking you. I never want to stop."

"Don't stop," she cried, her fingers stimulating her clit as he pounded her. "Oh, yes...I'm so close..."

He drew her head down, claiming her lips with his, his tongue swiping everywhere. Sucking her bottom lip through his teeth, he lightly clamped down. "Come all over my cock, baby. Come for me."

Joy's body bowed, the orgasm slamming through her body from the intoxicating combination of his deep voice, his sexy words and her own hand at her clit. Collapsing over his body, she let the convulsions take her, loving how he still pounded her quaking body.

He called her name, burying his face in her neck, and began to shoot his own release deep inside her core. Overcome with emotion, realizing it was most likely love, tears stung her eyes as she rejoiced in the beauty of what they had together. Never had she felt so close to someone while making love. It was beautiful and precious, and she was too wise to squander it.

Shuddering in his arms, Joy felt every inch of his warm embrace as his arms encircled her. Content to lay sprawled in his grasp forever, she squeezed her inner muscles around his shaft, hoping to intensify his pleasure as much as possible.

"Fuck, you're wringing me out, honey," he moaned into her neck.

"Mmmm..." she garbled into his skin. "Does it feel good?"

"Yes," he rasped, jerking below her. His hips thrust into hers, emitting the last jets of his release. "Oh, god..."

Sated, they clung to each other, breath labored as they fell back to Earth. Sam's hand lazily stroked the back of her head as she threaded her fingers through his hair atop the pillowcase. Unhurried and languid, they cherished each other's nearness, drifting into slumber in the dark February night until the first light of dawn filtered through her window. And then, Joy dragged him to the shower, where they loved each other all over again.

Chapter 14

Joy watched Sam throw on yesterday's clothes, admiring how sexy he was as he buttoned his shirt. Once he was finished, they padded to the kitchen where she whipped up two egg white omelets for them.

"Were you laughing at me while I dressed?" he asked, eyeing her suspiciously as she set the steaming omelet in front of him as he sat at the island counter.

"No," she said, finishing up her own eggs. "Well, yes. I was just laughing at how you'll be taking the walk of shame home. Usually, it's the girl, but you're draped in yesterday's clothing while I'm all snug in clean sweats."

His eyes sparkled as she sat on the stool beside him. Sipping coffee, he winked. "I'm thrilled to have been ravished by you, Ms. Paulson."

"Good," she said, stuffing a bite in her mouth. "I'll do it again soon."

He chuckled before his gaze grew concerned. "Are you okay? You winced."

"Oh, yeah," she said, waving a hand. "You're freaking huge, Sam. I'm just a bit sore. I haven't had sex in a long time."

His fingers encircled her wrist. "I'm sorry if I hurt you."

"Don't you dare apologize for boning my brains out. It was awesome. Believe me, it's well worth the slight discomfort the morning after."

He didn't look convinced. "Please just tell me if it's too much. I like hanging out with you, Joy. We don't have to have sex."

"That's sweet," she said, "but there's no way in hell you're getting out of banging me at every opportunity. Just so we're clear." She waggled her eyebrows.

He chuckled, shaking his head. "Well, if you insist..."

"Speaking of, I want to get this out in the open. I like you, Sam, and really care about you. I'm not interested in a random hook up here. I want to date you and have a relationship with you. I'd like to build something with you, just like we're building the business together. I know that's a lot, but I'm pretty direct, and I don't want things unsaid lingering between us."

The smile that had grown on his face as she'd spoken was now a full-on beam. "I've wanted to be your boyfriend for two years, Joy. It's nice you finally caught up."

She chewed thoughtfully, excited they were on the same page. "Is it weird that I'm older than you? I wasn't sure how old you were exactly, but I guessed thirty-ish. Now that I know you're twenty-nine, I'm feeling like a grandma over here."

"How old are you?" he asked, brows drawn together.

"Thirty-two. I'll be thirty-three in June."

"Wow. Do you need help with your walker? You're almost at the age where you're bound to break a hip," he teased.

"Stop it," she said, playfully swatting his arm. "I just want you to know what you're signing up for. I want it all, Sam. Marriage, kids, happily ever after. Not now, so don't freak out, but down the road. I'm telling you this so you understand what I'm looking for in a partner."

He grabbed her hand, bringing it to his lips and placing a kiss on the back. "I want all that stuff too. It was hard not having a family growing up and I've always wanted to create one that I belong to."

Joy felt tears burn her eyes. "You belong with our friend family. The girls and Carter love you. Oh, my god, I can't wait to tell them that we banged."

He laughed. "They'll be excited, huh?"

Nodding, she bit her lip, anticipation at seeing her friends' reaction coursing through her. "They're going to die."

"I really like them too," he said, grinning as he finished his breakfast. A bell chimed on Joy's phone and she picked it up to check the work email. Scrolling through, she felt her brow furrow.

"What's wrong?"

"Nothing. That new client, Martha Withers, needs to reschedule her two p.m. appointment today. Let me just message her back." Her fingers tapped across the screen as she sent an email offering alternate times the following week.

"That was my only appointment today," Sam said, leaning back and rubbing his now-full belly. "That means I can hang with you if you want me to." He looked so sweet, as if he thought she might say no.

Mulling it over, she said, "I'm heading to Long Island to see my mom today. I usually visit her once every few weeks on a Sunday. I know that isn't a lot, and you probably think I'm a horrible daughter, but she doesn't know who I am, and once I realized she would never remember me, visiting her became really hard."

Sam rested his hand on her shoulder, slowly stroking. "Then let me go with you."

Her eyes studied his, contemplating. "The visits with her aren't easy, Sam."

"Then I'd really like to go and support you through it."

Heart melting at the sincerity in his voice, she capitulated. "Okay. I need to get dressed and do a few things for SamJoy before we leave."

"I should probably put on some clean clothes," he said, giving her a sheepish grin. "Want to meet me at my apartment and then we can head to Penn Station together."

"You mean, I'm finally going to see your apartment? I was sure you were keeping those seven dead bodies in there."

"Very funny," he said, standing and placing a kiss on her head. "Should I wash the dishes before I go?"

"No, but I'm pretty sure you just earned 'best boyfriend of the year' status for asking. Holy shit. I have a freaking boyfriend. I mean, we did decide that, right?"

"Right," he said, leaning down and brushing her lips with his. "Now that I have you, I'm never letting you go. You're mine, Joy."

She shivered at the possessive words. "Promise?"

"Fuck yes." Drawing her to him, he gave her a thorough kiss. "Okay," he said, swiping a hand down her neck and squeezing. "I'll text you my exact address. Just ring the bell and I'll buzz you in."

"Be there around one. Can't wait to see where the magic happens."

He rolled his eyes as he shrugged on his coat. "You're making my life way more exciting than it is."

"Bye," she called as he walked out the door. Once the door was closed, she gave a squeal. Last night had been one of the most awesome of her life. Dying to tell her friends, she grabbed her phone and fell onto the cushions of the couch. She sent a text that she knew would knock them off their rockers in two seconds flat.

Joy: Ladies, I have an update: Sam's package does NOT disappoint.

Grinning, she waited for her phone to explode. It took less than twenty seconds. Answering the video call, Laura's face appeared on the screen.

"Oh, my god. Everything. Tell me. Now."

"Wait," Joy said, unable to control her laughter. "Kayla's calling in. Hold on." After accepting the call, both of their faces appeared onscreen.

"So, how many times did you bang? How big was his cock? Are you in looooove?" Laura asked.

"Yes, Joy, tell us *everything*," Carter mocked, his voice high pitched as he shoved his face into view over Kayla's.

"Damnit, Carter," Kayla said, face-palming him and pushing him out of the way. "Sorry, ladies. He's out of control right now. Okay, J, spill!"

So, Joy told them. About the amazing evening and the incredibly satisfying sex. Once she was finished, they both looked stunned.

"How could someone make it twenty-nine years without having sex? Holy crap, that's insane," Laura said.

"Not to me," Joy said, shrugging. "I think it shows how much being intimate with someone means to him. You guys know I've only had sex with four guys. Sam is my fifth. I mean, I'm still counting on one hand over here."

"I think it's sweet. Carter says I've made him a born-again virgin." Kayla snickered.

"You have. I've forgotten every woman but you, dear," Carter yelled from the kitchen.

Kayla rolled her eyes. "As if."

"Obviously keep this between us. I'm sure he doesn't want it to get out, but I had to tell you guys."

"Sure thing, J. And how did I suddenly become the loser in the group?" Laura asked. "You and Kayla have hot men with huge cocks and I have a vibrator that shorts out every other time I try to use it. What gives? Did I piss off the universe or something?"

"You still have us, sweetie," Joy said, "and it's going to happen for you. I promise. In the meantime, you both know you'll always be my true loves, deep in my heart."

"So true," Kayla said. "You guys are my freaking sisters. I love you so much."

"Okay, before I barf, I'll say that I love you both too, but I'm still rampantly jealous and might never forgive you." Laura's warm smile negated the teasing words. "Are you going to see your mom today, J?"

"Yes," she nodded. "Sam's coming with me."

"That's sweet," Kayla said.

"By the way, any pointers from Kevin about the deposition next week? I want to be prepared." Joy said.

Kayla sighed. "He says it's going to be tough. The evidence you gave him—all the emails and documents that Drake manipulated—Drake is claiming you doctored them on your end after he informed you they were imperfect."

"That's ridiculous!" Joy said, sitting up on the couch. "He's such a fucking liar."

"I know, sweetie," Kayla said. "The law sucks because you need to have irrefutable proof. It would really help if we had something that shows malicious intent, not just a 'he said, she said' scenario. But don't worry. We'll keep fighting. We'll take it all the way to trial if we have to, although Kevin says these employment cases usually end up settling out of court."

"Well, I hope we can stick it to that bastard," Joy said. "What a jerk."

"But look at the silver lining," Laura said wistfully. "Without being fired, you never would've started spending all this time with Sam, and then you never would've been ravished by his amazing cock."

Joy giggled. "You sound like an optimist, Laura. How refreshing."

"Uggh," she said, rolling her eyes. "You two lovebirds have turned me into a sap. I've gotta go. My dead vibrator is calling. Byeeeee. It will all work out, Joy. Love you ladies!"

"Bye, sweetie," Kayla said. "I'll keep you updated. For now, don't worry. Good luck with your mom today."

"Thanks, K."

Anger coursed through Joy as she clicked off the phone. Frustrated that Drake might actually win, she stomped to the bedroom to get dressed. Telling herself that a prick like Drake didn't deserve her energy, she vowed to focus on the good things in her life, like her burgeoning relationship with Sam.

Chapter 15

S am opened the door, nervousness causing his palms to sweat as Joy observed his home. He lived in a two-bedroom on the second floor of a recently renovated building. When he'd moved in three years ago, the place had been spotless and Sam strived to keep it so. He was a bit of a clean freak and thought Joy would appreciate that since she was always lamenting about her OCD.

She walked over to the large black chair in front of his TV, outfitted with controllers and wires. "What's this?" she asked.

"It's a gaming chair," he said, feeling his face flush about a thousand shades of red. "I enjoy gaming and that makes it easier to have one home base for controlling multiple avatars."

She gave him a mischievous smile. "It looks big enough for me to sit on your lap while you play."

Laughing, he nodded. "Probably, but if you're over here, I'm damn sure not going to be focused on video games."

"I've never played before, except Sega when I was really young. Maybe you can teach me one day?"

Sam swallowed. "You want to learn how to play video games?"

Approaching him, she slid her palms over his pecs, covered by his dress shirt. "I want to learn to do things that you like. So, if you like gaming, I want you to teach me."

Drawing her to him, he slid his arms around her waist. Lowering his head, he brushed her lips with his. "I have no idea why, but that's incredibly hot."

She kissed him, gently running her tongue over his bottom lip. "I can even play naked if you ask me nicely."

"Holy shit," he breathed, consuming her mouth as he imagined her pale skin glowing in the stark chair. Their tongues mated as he lost himself in the vision, dying to make it a reality.

"One day, big boy," she breathed into his mouth. "That's a promise."

He rested his forehead on hers, disbelief coursing through him that this was now his reality. Somehow, he'd actually ended up snagging Joy. The one woman he feared he could never have and now craved more than his lungs needed air. Awash in thankfulness, he nudged her nose with his. "I like this," he whispered.

"I like it too," she said. Her fingers stroked the back of his neck, under his hairline. "When we get back, we'll have some sexy times. For now, you ready to head to the Island?"

"Ready," he said, drawing back and taking her hand. After donning his coat, he led her out of the apartment and down the stairs, pulling up a rideshare app on his phone.

"We can take the train," she said.

He shrugged. "Let's just take an Uber. It can't be too much on a Sunday. Then, I can get you home faster."

She helped him pull up the address of the assisted living home in Western Nassau County and they were on their way. The twenty-five-minute drive was easy, devoid of traffic, and they chatted amicably with their driver about his Valentine's date the previous evening. It hadn't gone very well and Sam thought Joy so cute as she snickered at his recap.

"And how was your evening?" the driver asked, eyeing them in the rear-view mirror. "It seems that it was better than mine. You two have the look of being happy lovers."

"We are happy lovers," she said, reaching over and squeezing his hand. Sam clenched back, threading his fingers through hers. A sudden chill washed over him, one that he remembered from all those years ago when the police had shown up at his neighbor's house to tell them the news. They had been babysitting him the night his parents died and he remembered the officers' expressionless faces, even though he'd been so young. Everything he'd known had been gone in a flash. Could that happen with him and Joy? Telling himself he was being irrational, he inhaled a deep, calming breath.

"You okay, there?" she asked.

"Fine," he said. "I'm excited to meet your mom."

"Don't expect much," she said, sadness lacing her tone. "But I'm happy you're meeting her too."

Once they reached the facility, they entered a large sitting room through the front door. A young nurse sat beside a woman who was in a wheelchair, covered with a knitted blanket.

"Hi, Kara," Joy said to the nurse. "How's she doing today?"

"Fine," Kara said, standing. "She actually ate some breakfast this morning."

"That's good," Joy said. "This is my boyfriend, Sam. Sam, this is my mother's nurse, Kara. She's a godsend and is assigned exclusively to my mom and two other dementia patrons here at the home. My sister and I couldn't do this without her."

"It's my pleasure," Kara said, shaking Sam's hand. "You know I love Carol. She's in a good mood today." Leaning down, Kara said in a loud voice. "Carol? Your daughter Joy is here. Can you tell her hello?"

Carol's gaze drifted upward, her eyes the same light blue as Joy's. "I don't know anyone named Joy," she rasped.

"It's me, Mom," Joy said, taking her hand.

Carol pulled it free, giving a loud cry. "Don't touch me. Where is George?"

"George isn't here today. It's just me and Sam. Would you like to meet Sam?"

Carol remained stubbornly quiet as she sat in the unmoving chair.

Sighing, Joy said to Kara, "Why don't you grab something to eat. We'll wheel her around outside the facility for a while to get her blood moving." Kara nodded and trailed away.

"Mom, this is Sam," Joy said, pointing to him.

"It's a pleasure to meet you, Mrs. Paulson," Sam said, compassion welling in his chest. She stared at his outstretched hand.

"You have my George's hands," Carol said softly.

Joy gave him a heartbreaking smile. "George was my dad," she said, her eyes full of grief as she stared up at him. "I guess we Paulson women have a thing for hands."

Sam wanted to pull Joy into his body and hold her until she never hurt again. Instead, he crouched down and offered his hand, palm up, to Carol. "You can shake it if you like. I'm not George but, judging by the amazing daughter you both raised, I'm sure I would've liked him."

Carol's cobalt irises dragged over him until she gingerly slid her frail palm over his and shook.

"Wow," Joy said. "I've haven't seen her voluntarily touch someone in years. That's amazing."

"It's an honor to meet you, Mrs. Paulson."

"Thank you, George. You should ask me to dance."

"Should I?" he asked, rising to his full height as he disengaged his hand from hers. "I can see where you get your directness from."

Joy chuckled. "It's how they met. She used to tell the story all the time. Dad was apparently in love with some hussy from their high school but Mom was determined to marry him so she forced him to ask her to dance."

"Yikes. I'm finding that I'm very intimidated by the Paulson women."

"They were high school sweethearts," Joy said wistfully. "It's really cute."

"It is," he said, unable to resist sliding his arms around her shoulders and pulling her to his side. "Should we go on a walk?"

"Yes," she said, reaching down to unlock the wheels of the chair. "The place is actually really pretty. Let's do it."

The sun shone brightly on the brisk day as they pushed Carol along the paved sidewalks of the facility for a while before heading back inside and wheeling her down the various hallways. After about an hour, they met Kara in Carol's room. Joy discussed the details of the next week's care with the kind nurse before they left. She was quiet in the Uber home and Sam drew her to his side, content to let her rest against him as she mulled the visit.

Once back at his apartment, they decided to order in and chill.

"Is it okay if I stay here tonight?" she asked. "Your first appointment is at nine a.m., so I can head home when you get up."

"I'd love that," he said, placing his phone on the counter now that the food had been ordered. "There's a new fantasy show streaming that we can watch. Spoiler alert: if you try to seduce me on the couch, I might actually let you this time."

She threw her head back, giving her first full laugh since they'd visited her mother, causing his heart to swell. "Was it that obvious I was trying to seduce you when I fell asleep in your lap?"

"Yes," he said, tugging her to the couch. "I was dumb enough to resist you. What was I thinking?"

They found the show and watched a bit until the food came. After eating, Sam gave her a t-shirt and an old pair of boxers so she could relax.

"These are huge," she said, walking out of his room, looking adorable in the oversized clothing. Striding over to him, she crawled on top of him, straddling his lap. "Good thing I might let you take them off me if you're a good boy."

He nipped her lips, his shaft already hard as it strained through the sweat pants he'd recently changed into. "How good?" he murmured.

"Mmmm..." she said, digging her nails into the back of his neck. "Maybe I don't want you to be good at all."

He snagged her lips in a heated kiss, tugging the bottom lip through his teeth over and over as she squirmed. "I want to eat your pussy, honey."

She stilled, leaning back, eyes wide as they slowly blinked. "Wow," she said. "That's pretty blunt."

"Sorry," he said, feeling like an idiot. "You said you like dirty talk, but I think I'm really bad at it. But I do want to kiss you here," he said, cupping her mound. "I'm not very experienced at it, but I'll do my damnedest to make it good for you."

"First of all," she said, pushing her core into his hand, "you're awesome at dirty talk. It's just going to take me a while to get used to it." She pecked him on the lips. "And, second, you can definitely kiss me there. *Hell*, yes. I'm sure it will be good. If I need something, I'll tell you, okay?"

He nodded before lifting her, reveling in her high-pitched yelp, as he repositioned her on the cushions. Her wispy hair fanned over the arm of his couch and he shook his head. "You're so fucking pretty, Joy."

"Thank you," she said shyly.

"Don't get bashful on me now, honey," he said, lowering to his knees beside the couch. "Take off your shirt."

"Yes, sir," she rasped, grasping the hem and dragging it over her head before tossing it to the floor.

Sam sucked in a breath. "You're not wearing a bra."

"I took it off when I changed," she said, biting her lip.

"Slide your hands over your breasts," he said, unaware of where the dominant command came from but feeling the need to be in control somewhere deep inside.

Wide eyes locked with his, she slid her hands slowly up her stomach, palming the small globes. Sam's heartbeat quickened, his breathing choppy and erratic. "Pinch your nipples," he growled.

She complied, eliciting a soft groan from him as she squished the tender flesh between her thumbs and forefingers.

"Fuck," he whispered, leaning down to kiss her. After devouring her lips, he kissed a trail down her chin, across the base of her neck and between her breasts. Encircling her wrist, he drew her hand to his head. "Pull my hair," he said, loving how her nipple puckered beneath his warm breath. "I realized last night that it drives me fucking crazy when you pull my hair while I kiss your nipples."

Her fingers entwined in his hair, gently tugging, sending sparks of desire to his cock. Lowering his lips, he surrounded her nipple and began to pull. Showering the tiny bud with affection, he swiped his tongue over it, then flicked it with the tip, back and forth, as she writhed below him.

He dragged her other hand to his head and she latched it in his hair, drawing his mouth to her other nipple as her back arched.

"Sam..." she wailed as he grunted against her skin.

The bud of her nipple was the sweetest candy to his starving tongue. Lathering it, he slathered it with his saliva, marking her in the most primal way, before lightly biting it. Her body bowed off the couch as she screamed his name, lost to pleasure, and he wanted to weep with delight. If he could spend the rest of his days pleasing her, it would never be enough.

Gliding his hand down her abdomen, he slid it under the hem of the shorts, searching for her folds. Finding them, he drew his finger down her center, circling the entrance to her wet channel.

"Yes..." she hissed, pushing her hips toward his hand. "I want your fingers inside me, Sam."

He speared them into her, still sucking her nipple as he watched her reaction. She shuddered, eyes closing as she purred. "So fucking good," she wailed. "Don't stop."

He worked her with two fingers, scissoring them around her wet walls as she seemed to drown in pleasure. Dying to taste her, he shifted lower and all but ripped the shorts from her quivering body. Palming her inner thighs, he pushed her legs open, baring her pussy. It glistened before him, wet and swollen, and he almost came in his pants. Lowering his face between her legs, he inhaled her scent, rubbing the tip of his nose along one of her folds.

"I'm dead," she moaned, head thrown back on the arm of the couch. "You're killing me."

Channeling everything he'd ever learned about oral sex, he touched the surface of his tongue to her opening, tasting the essence that was Joy. Circling it, he stimulated the muscles at the opening of her core before spearing his tongue inside.

"Oh, god..." she cried, clutching his head and drawing him further into her center. He impaled her with his tongue, deep and thorough, lathering her until her body was shaking so violently, he wondered if she was close to coming. Wanting to make that happen, he slid his tongue up to her clit, searching for the tiny nub.

"Pull me open," she said, groaning. "It will give you better access." Following her direction, he pulled the swollen folds apart, latching his tongue to her clit and alternating between flicking it with the tip and sucking it between his lips.

"Holy crap," she said, her hips undulating as she gyrated against his face. "I'm gonna come...oh, Sam...oh, yes!"

She exploded beneath him, crashing into his tongue as her hips gyrated. Closing his warm mouth over her, he sucked until she clutched his hair, which he now knew meant she couldn't take any more stimulation. Watching her, his face buried in her sweet pussy, a deep wave of pleasure overtook him as she convulsed. Seeing her flushed frame come from his ministrations did all sorts of things to his own body. Dying to bury himself in her, he let her ride the wave.

Eventually, her shudders turned to slight trembles and he began to slither over her body.

"No way, buddy," she said, eyes snapping open as she placed a palm on his chest. "Pull out that magnificent cock and get inside me. Now."

Sam was no fool. Jerking down his pants, he grabbed her hips, pulling her toward the edge of the couch. Rising on his knees, he aligned the head of his cock with her damp opening.

Gaze cemented to hers, he impaled her with one thrust, desperate to feel her around him. She lay limp, mewling with desire, allowing him full control of their loving. Taking advantage, he slapped his body against hers mercilessly, reveling in the feel of his balls against her ass each time he slammed into her.

"So good," she moaned, the words stilted and broken as she lay sated on the couch. "Oh, Sam, it's so good with you."

"I know, baby," he gritted, unable to unclench his teeth, trying like hell to hold off the orgasm that threatened to burst from his straining body. "I love being inside you."

Heart threatening to pound out of his chest from exertion, he pummeled her until he felt his balls tighten. Moving at a maddening pace, he fucked her with every last ounce of will until he couldn't resist any longer. Bellowing her name, he began to pulse jets of release deep inside her warmth, each burst signaling his claim on her, his beautiful Joy. His woman. *His.*

I love you. The words flitted through his brain and he had to struggle to keep them inside. What they had was new, and he didn't want to ruin it by professing love like an inexperienced dolt. He'd already experienced enough embarrassment at being a virgin and definitely didn't need a vow of unrequited love hanging between them.

Unable to balance on his knees, he fell over her soft body, head nestling between her breasts as his shaft relaxed inside her tight channel.

"Good grief," she breathed, threading her fingers through his hair. "You're amazing at oral sex. Check. I'm beginning to doubt that you were really a virgin."

Sam chuckled, placing a tender kiss on the curve of her breast. "I'm so glad I could make you come that way. You taste so good, honey. It's unbelievable."

"Thank goodness you think so. Some guys don't like doing that."

He lifted his head, eyebrows drawn together. "Are they insane?"

Laughing, she shrugged. "I don't know, but I'm really happy you seem to enjoy it."

"Oh, hell yes, I enjoy it." Straightening, he ran his hands over her hips and upper thighs. "You have bruises here." Lifting his gaze to hers, he felt his heart plummet in his chest. "Did I bruise you?"

"It's okay," she said, running her fingers over his bicep. "You grab me pretty hard when you're slamming that amazing cock inside me."

"Damnit," he said, trailing his fingertips over the tiny blue-black marks that mimicked the grip of his fingers. "I'm so sorry. I feel terrible."

"Do you see me complaining?" she asked. Wriggling on the pillows, she attempted to sit up and Sam pulled her to a sitting position, his shaft still inside her. Palming his face, she smiled. "I like it when you're dominant. That was so sexy. I bruise really easily and don't mind it. If you hurt me, I'll tell you, okay?"

"You have to tell me, Joy," he said, seriousness emanating from his firm tone. "I can't live with myself if I hurt you."

"I know," she said, running her thumb across his lip. "I'll tell you, but I don't want you holding back. Promise?"

"I'm a big guy, Joy. If I need to hold back, I will."

"No," she said, cupping his chin. "I need you to let go with me. Trust me, Sam. This won't work if you don't."

"Sweetheart—"

"Trust me," she interrupted.

Sighing, he ran his fingers through the hair at her temple. "Okay," he finally said.

"Now, I think we're starting to slip here. Wanna carry me to the bathroom and clean me up? I'm suddenly starving again and dying for leftovers."

Studying her trusting blue eyes, he realized she spoke the truth and was fine. Although, he would certainly be more cognizant of how he handled her soft skin in the future. Cupping her outer thighs, he drew them to encircle his waist before lifting her, loving that he was still inside her. Even though his shaft was sated, it was still large enough to rest inside her as he carried her to the bathroom. She clutched him close, adding to the feeling that they were one.

Sam had never felt so complete.

They settled in, relaxing on the couch until it grew late, and then holding each other as they fell asleep in Sam's king-sized bed. As he drifted, her head on his chest, all he could think was that he'd finally found his person.

Sam, who'd lost his family when he was so young, was finally whole.

Chapter 16

S am and Joy settled into a routine, their business growing alongside their flourishing romance. Joy found herself loving the pace of the new business. Her days were filled with scheduling appointments for Sam, managing the books, and researching and employing what marketing tactics would work best for SamJoy. Sam had given her a marketing budget of twenty thousand dollars from his investment account, but she was adamant about only using half, if that. She felt that, if she researched correctly, she could generate a high return-on-investment for the ads without costing them a fortune.

Facebook and Google ads seemed to work the best, and she also reached out to some local business podcast hosts. Not only were their ads reasonable, but several of the hosts invited Sam to appear on the broadcast and promote his business. Joy couldn't help but laugh at his horrified expression as she told him one evening, a few weeks after Valentine's Day.

"Joy," he said, shaking his head as he sat beside her on the couch, munching the pizza they'd ordered—cheese-free for Sam since he was lactose intolerant. "I can't go on a podcast. What part of 'I'm incredibly shy and would fumble everything' don't you get?"

"You're not *that* shy," she said, squishing her feet into his thigh as her back rested against the arm of the couch. "You were always somewhat talkative with me at RMG."

"I always said the dumbest stuff around you," he said, rolling his eyes. "I was sure you thought I was incapable of speaking English half the time."

"No way," she said, winking. "You were always so sweet. I know you can do this, Sam. It will be great exposure for SamJoy."

"Only if you come on with me," he muttered.

"Right," she said, thinking he was joking.

"I'm serious," he said, eyes wide with sincerity. "We're partners, Joy. If I'm going to face my embarrassment head-on, I need you by my side. You'll bring a personality to the interview that I just don't possess."

"I don't know..." Her eyebrows drew together. "I guess that could work."

"Good," he said, patting her leg and squeezing her calf. "We'll do it together. Thank goodness. And great job even thinking of podcasts. That's really smart."

She snuggled into the couch, glowing from his praise. In reality, Sam was one of the most intelligent people she'd ever met. His knowledge of tech and finance was unrivaled in her mind. She'd always been slightly ashamed for not finishing her bachelor's degree, feeling it made her less worthy in the eyes of some, but Sam truly appeared to think her knowledgeable and creative. It was just another in the long list of reasons that he'd captured her heart.

As the weeks wore on, winter turned to a chilly spring, and Joy's case against Drake and RMG progressed. It wasn't going as well as Joy had hoped, but she remained optimistic, telling herself that a jerk like Drake would never win. The world still had enough good in it that guys like him lost in the end, didn't it?

By the end of April, Sam had recruited Will and Jamal to work as independent contractors for SamJoy. Joy thought them both lovely and agreed to join their monthly card game at Sam's house at the beginning of May.

"I taught her how to play, guys," Sam said, shuffling the cards above the green felt of the table, "so tread lightly. She's a shark."

"Don't worry," Joy said, waggling her eyebrows at their guests. "I'll only take ninety percent of your money. I'll leave you with a ten percent cut to get a taxi home."

The five of them played, laughter filling the air as Frank caught Sam up on everything at RMG. Since he was the IT supervisor, he'd decided to stay, and Joy couldn't blame him. It was a stable job and he seemed to enjoy it. Sadly, after only an hour, she was out, Sam taking the last of her chips as he guiltily turned over his hand.

"Full house," he said, his red cheeks so handsome, encased in his sheepish expression. "I'm sorry, honey."

"You cad," she teased, shoving her chips toward him. "I have no choice but to deny you my favors forever."

"Take them back," he said, pushing all his chips toward her, causing the guys to laugh. "You can have them all. Whatever you want."

Chuckling, she stood and pushed them back his way. Placing a kiss on his thick hair, she squeezed his shoulder. "I'm going to make myself useful and heat up some appetizers for us. I'm starving. Who needs a refill?"

Mumbles accompanied raised hands and Joy shuffled into Sam's kitchen to prepare the food. Since they were playing in his second bedroom, she could hear muffled conversation as she prepared everything.

As she approached the door to the room, she froze, hearing her name in their hushed conversation.

"Come on, man," Jamal said. "Now that you've finally gotten laid, you can't stop with just one chick. We need to live vicariously through you. You can't seriously want to only sleep with one woman for the rest of your life, right? Don't you want to know what it feels like to be with someone else before you close that door?'

"No way," Sam said, causing Joy's lips to curve. "Joy is it for me guys."

"Are you guys really that serious?" Frank asked. "And, anyway, who knows what's going to happen? I'd say keep your options open, dude. You never know."

"Seriously, Sam," Will said. "Eventually, you're going to wonder what it's like with someone else. Joy's great, but I don't want you waking up one day realizing you sacrificed the opportunity to experience being with other women. Just think about it."

Silence permeated the room, the only sound that of chips being counted. Finally, Sam said, "You're right, guys. It's certainly limiting to only be with one person your entire life. I'll think about it. You in, Will? If not, I'm going to raise."

Joy's breath shot from her lungs, hurt spreading through her frame. She hadn't even considered that Sam might want to experience sex with other women. After all, he wasn't even thirty yet and had so much life yet to live. Was she denying him the opportunity to gain something he needed?

Doubt hummed through her veins as she dispersed the apps and beer, never indicating she'd overheard the conversation. As the night progressed, she toiled around on her laptop as the guys played, unable to shake the uncertainty. Around eleven, the game wrapped, Sam the victor, and his friends shuffled out the door. After saying her goodbyes, Joy headed into the bathroom, filled with a steely sense of determination. Applying the lustrous, silky pink gloss, she gave her reflection a nod. Stalking into Sam's bedroom, she found him shirtless, pulling off his pants.

"Hey," he said, his gorgeous smile turning her insides to liquid. "Thanks for being so great tonight. The guys love you."

Striding toward him, she grabbed the pants from his hand, tossing them to the chair. "Take your underwear off and lay down," she said, her voice gravelly.

His eyes widened and he followed her command, yanking off his boxer briefs before lying on the bed, threading his hands behind his head on the pillow.

She started slowly undressing, sliding her shirt off before gradually unzipping her jeans and gliding them down her legs.

"I put on extra lip gloss tonight," she said, unclasping her bra and letting it slide seductively to the ground. "By the time I'm done with you, it's going to cover every inch of your body. Would you like that?"

"Yes," he rasped. His cock twitched on his toned abdomen, sending a rush of moisture between her thighs.

Removing her underwear and dropping it on the floor, she slid her silky leg over his, straddling his stomach.

"You're already wet," he said, pushing his belly into her core. "I can feel it."

Leaning down, she brushed her lips over his, glossing them with the sticky substance. "That's what you do to me, Sam," she said, kissing him ever so gently. "You're everything I've ever wanted in a lover."

"So are you," he groaned, lifting his hand to spear his fingers through the hair at the top of her neck.

She wasn't quite sure about that anymore, but she was determined to show him she could fulfill him. That she was the *only* woman he needed.

"Uh-uh," she said, grasping his wrist and directing it back toward his head. "No touching tonight. Keep your hands above your head. I'm going to taste every part of you."

"I want to touch you," he whispered.

She shook her head, smiling mischievously as she slid her damp core over his stomach. "Be a good boy and let me rock your world."

"Oh, god," he rasped.

She captured his lips with hers, spearing her tongue into his mouth as he groaned. He kissed her back with all the ardor she'd come to expect from her Sam, his loving always so generous and passionate. Trailing kisses to his ear, she blew warm breath into the shell as he shivered under her.

He called her name as she extended the tip of her tongue into the sensitive crevice, dragging it around the shell until she bit the lobe. Sucking it through her teeth, she bit down lightly, showing him she was in the mood to suck several parts of his body with her shimmering lips.

"Fuck," he said, his arms lifting, surrounding her as she lapped the sensitive lobe of his ear.

Rising above him, she grasped his wrists, pushing them down beside his head, holding him captive underneath her aroused body. "No hands," she warned.

"Okay, baby," he said, looking slightly chastised. The expression was adorable. God, she loved this man. Realization rushed through her as she accepted what she'd known for some time now: she was deeply in love with Sam. It was a poignant moment, especially when her body was throbbing with need. How magnificent that she would fall in love with a man who was so kind, thoughtful *and* sexy. Vowing not to squander it, she resumed her torturous loving.

Giving him one more stern glare, she inched down his body, causing him to groan when her wet core settled over his shaft. Lowering her head, she pressed her lips to his nipple. As she licked it with her glistening tongue, her fingers toyed with his other nipple, pinching and tweaking as he squirmed under her.

"Honey, that feels so good, but if I don't get inside you soon, I'm going to come."

Eyes locked with his, she kissed a trail from one of his nipples to the other, making sure to leave a smattering of the pink gloss behind. Extending her tongue, she lathered his nipple, loving how it hardened under her lips, the evidence of his desire sending rushes of arousal through her flushed body.

His hand drifted toward his chest, the pad of his finger rubbing the trail of gloss as her mouth worked his nipple. "So fucking hot," he said, stroking the sticky substance that now covered the tiny hairs between his nipples. Lifting his finger, he brought it to her lips. Joy lifted her chin, letting him circle her swollen lips with his finger. "How are you so pretty?" he murmured.

Joy opened her mouth, inviting him in. Taking her direction, he slid his finger between her lips. Closing her mouth, she moved back and forth, sucking his finger, showing him what she was ready to do to his straining cock. She reveled in the arousal simmering in his crystal irises as he watched her through heavy lids.

Sliding her tongue up his wet finger, she popped it free from her lips. Rising to her knees, she traced butterfly kisses down his toned abs, stopping at his navel to dip her tongue into the tiny crevice. His hips bucked as he groaned her name. Grasping his cock in her hand, Joy studied him in the dim light of the bedside lamp. Her hand barely covered half his engorged cock, the veins under the tender skin full with arousal. Lowering her head, she touched her lips to his aching shaft, running them from the base to the head, slathering him with the silky gloss. Done with her demand that he not use his hands, Sam thrust his fingers into her hair, clutching as his hips undulated beneath her.

"I'm sorry, sweetheart," he said, his breath labored. "I have to touch you."

She nodded, sliding her lips back down his cock. With her free hand, she palmed his balls, eliciting a deep, sensual moan from his throat. "Oh, god, honey."

After gently massaging his balls, she glided her lips to them, spreading the glittery substance over the sensitive flesh. Gently sucking the delicate skin into her mouth, she watched him writhe.

"Please, baby," he pleaded, fingers scrunching her hair.

Smiling, she observed her handiwork. "You're sparkly all over now," she said, biting her lip.

"I won't have any dreams left," he said, his gaze so reverent. "You make them all come true."

Inwardly sighing, she wondered if she'd ever heard anything so romantic. Deciding that impossible, she thanked the heavens for placing her in Sam's path. What a gift he was to her. Grinning, she grasped his cock. "I'm going to kiss you here until you come in my mouth, okay?"

"I want to come inside your pussy," he said softly, tracing his finger along her jaw.

"We'll do that later," she said, shifting over him. "Let me love you this way."

His eyes darted back and forth between hers. "Okay," he whispered.

Lifting his cock from his stomach, she cemented her gaze to his. Joy wanted to drown in those hazel eyes as she gave him pleasure. Drawing him to her lips, she closed her mouth around him and slid over the straining flesh.

Since he was so large, there was no way she could take all of him into her mouth. Letting the saliva drip down his shaft, she used it to facilitate jerking the base of his cock with her hand. Eyes never leaving his, she trailed her tongue over his flesh, working her wet mouth to the tip and back down, loving his guttural groans and growls. His hips jutted toward her face, working in tandem with her movements, and she purred around his skin.

Her cheeks hollowed, creating even more suction, and his fingers tightened to the point of pleasure-pain in her hair. It was erotic to Joy, knowing her actions were throwing him off balance, making him crazed with desire.

"I'm going to come, honey," he cried, looking so damn sexy as his body quaked beneath her. She nodded around his cock, urging him on, the gyrations of her mouth and hand frantic and strong.

Screaming her name, his body bucked, and warm, pulsing jets of release began spurting against the back of her throat. She'd loved him this way before, but he'd never come in her mouth, and she swallowed the salty substance, exalting in the taste of him on her tongue. It elicited a visceral reaction deep in her core, causing her own body to flush with wetness as she felt marked by him in a whole new way. Reveling in the uncontrolled shudders of his body, she felt pride that she could elicit such a response. It was intimate and sensual, and she felt connected to him, as she always did when they made love.

Finally, his body was replete, and his hand relaxed in her hair. "Crap," he murmured, gently massaging her scalp where he'd so recently tugged the strands. "Are you okay? Was I too rough?"

Smiling, she slowly slid up his body, lying atop his flushed frame as she placed a tender kiss on his lips. "It was perfect. I love having you inside me. Anywhere. Everywhere."

"Joy," he said, his gaze so adoring as he softly stroked her cheek, she felt her heart might burst.

"I know," she whispered, snuggling into his body and burying her head in the curve of his neck. "I know, Sam."

Content to stay entwined in his arms for the rest of the night, she let him hold her as his body still softly trembled.

Chapter 17

As the brisk winds of early spring turned to sunnier days in late May, Joy was focused on ensuring the business continued its strong growth through the summer. As she sat at her desk working on various marketing solutions, her phone rang.

"Hi, Kayla," she said through the tiny Bluetooth receiver on her ear.

"Hey, sweetie. I've got Kevin on the phone with me too."

"Hi, Joy," Kevin's deep voice said. "I wanted to discuss your case."

"Okay," she said, sitting straighter in her chair as worry took hold deep in her belly.

"Unfortunately, we've compiled all the evidence and both depositions. First, let me say that I believe you one hundred percent. Drake was quite hostile during his deposition and he gave many statements that I feel are false. Although that may be the case, we don't have enough evidence to take this to trial. It's the classic case of differing versions of a story. If you had any evidence showing malicious intent, we could build a much stronger case but, for now, we're going to have to try and settle. At best, you'll probably only get your legal fees back."

Joy felt deflated, unable to comprehend how there was any justice in the situation.

"Kevin and I are going to work together to create the best settlement package we can, Joy," Kayla said. "I promise, we'll do our best to bury these jerks."

They discussed more details, Joy feeling numb the entire time until Kevin signed off.

"You okay, J?" Kayla asked. "I'm worried about you."

"I'm fine," she said, feeling anything but. "I'll see you at Laura's event tonight, right?"

"Yep. Carter and I should be there by six-thirty. Thank goodness it's on a Tuesday since that's his night off."

"Sam is meeting us there around that time. He's coming straight from his last appointment. I'll see you there."

"Okay," Kayla said, her tone laced with concern. "Don't let this get you down, J. We're gonna grill those bastards. Have hope."

Sighing, Joy ended the call, racking her brain for any further evidence she could supply to help prove she was the injured party in her case against Drake. Pulling up her email, she did various searches, trying to find something new, or perhaps something she'd forgotten to give to Kevin, but it had all been turned over.

An idea popped into her head and she pulled up Sam's personal email, which she had access to along with his calendar and phone as SamJoy's business manager. She knew that he'd emailed himself several work documents before leaving RMG, and wondered if there was anything at all that implicated Drake. It was a long shot, but Joy was desperate.

After searching various words, she inputted "Drake" and "Joy" into the email search bar. A few things popped up, mostly about the form to replace her old work computer, but one stood out from the rest. Stopping her scroll, the mouse arrow hovered across an email with the subject, **Screen Shot Drake Email About Joy**. Eyes narrowing, she clicked. As she read, a huge cloud of disbelief encompassed her entire body.

Remember the bet we had about who could bang our executive assistant first? I asked Joy out and I totally thought she'd say yes. She can't look away when I do curls in the office and I know she wants to fuck me. But she said no, the little bitch. Guess I'm losing this one. How about we go double or nothing on the hottest chick that works in our building? There's this hot one on the third floor who I see every time I get coffee. She'd totally suck my dick. Let me know if you're in. By the way, Joy really pissed me off. I'm going to have to find a way to fire her. Imagine someone like that mousy little twit rejecting me. Whore.

Joy read the email over and over, not understanding how Sam could've kept something so important from her. Noting the date, she realized it was sent several days before her firing, meaning that Sam knew Drake was out to terminate her and did nothing. He didn't alert HR and he certainly didn't tell Joy. Why? Racking her brain, she deliberated how someone she trusted so deeply could keep something of this magnitude from her.

Eventually, the shock grew into hurt, and the hurt evolved to anger. Furious that Sam had intentionally deceived her, she reached for her phone, intent on confronting him. Before she made the call, she checked herself. Discussing something this important shouldn't be done over the phone. Deciding to discuss it later, after Laura's event, she simmered in her anger and frustration, contemplating if she really knew Sam at all.

S am rushed to get to Laura's fashion event, inwardly admitting he knew absolutely nothing about the clothing world but wanting to support her. She, Kayla and Carter had become true friends over the months he'd been dating Joy, and he was always thrilled to support a friend.

As he entered the door of the fancy Upper East Side boutique, Laura thrust a glass of champagne in his hand. "Well, well, our male model is here."

"Right," Sam said, sardonically. "I don't think I've ever been in a store this nice." He observed the fancy, shimmery clothing hanging on various racks. "I'm lost."

"You'll do fine. Now that my personal stylist business is up and running, I have to do silly events like this to attract new clients. It sure beats working as a buyer for big stores, which I did for way too long. I like working for myself. I'm sure you can appreciate that."

"I can," he said, sipping the champagne. "Is Joy here?"

"She's in the back with Kayla and Carter. I told her that you guys can hide, but I do need you to come out of the corner every once in a while and tell the shoppers I'm the best personal stylist you've ever met."

"Can do," he said, grinning, "since you're the *only* personal stylist I've ever met."

"Touché," she said, arching a brow. "Leave that part out, will ya? See you in a bit." She sauntered off, looking like a million dollars with her straight, silky black hair and athletic body draped in fabric that looked rather expensive. Searching for Joy, he located her and headed to the back.

"Hey, guys," he said, pulling his laptop bag from his shoulder and setting the champagne on the small, high top round table. Smiling at Joy, he lowered to give her a kiss. As he pecked her lips, he sensed something was off. Her eyes lacked their ever-present sparkle and her shoulders were stiff. "You okay?" he murmured.

"Fine," she said, her tone gruff. "I need to speak to you about something when we get home, but not here."

Dread coursed through him. Had he pissed her off somehow? Or worse, hurt her in some way? As his heartbeat accelerated, he racked his brain, searching for what he could've done to anger her.

"Let's go chat up those rich looking old broads," Kayla said, grabbing Joy's hand. "I bet they could use a personal stylist and they look wealthy as shit."

The ladies trailed away, leaving Sam with Carter. Sighing, he imbibed another sip of champagne.

"You're in trouble, dude," Carter said, eyeing the room. "I don't know what you did, but it dropped about a hundred degrees when you walked into the store."

"I know," Sam said, rubbing the back of his neck. "Damnit, I must've done something stupid, but I have no idea what it was."

Carter slapped him on the shoulder. "Take it from me, man, just suck it up and apologize. Chicks close down shop and refuse to reopen until you tell them you're sorry about a thousand times. If you ever want to get laid again, don't stop apologizing. Especially now, since you waited so long. I love Kayla to death, but she wears the pants. I've never had to work so hard to get someone to forgive me when I fuck up." He broke into a huge smile. "But she always does, eventually, and we have amazing makeup sex. Hell, it almost makes every fight worth it."

Sam swallowed thickly, a slight ringing in his ears. "Good advice, thanks. What did you mean about me waiting so long?"

Carter shrugged. "You know, since Joy's the first woman you've been with. I told you, man, these girls tell each other everything."

Sam's lungs slammed in his chest as realization washed over him. Struggling to breathe, he comprehended that Joy had told her friends about the secret that caused him so much embarrassment and shame. Humiliated, he felt his face flush as his hands trembled in shock.

"It's okay, Sam," Carter said, his tone laced with compassion. "It's nothing to be ashamed of. I wish that Kayla was the only woman I'd ever been with. I was an idiot before I met her. Joy's an amazing woman and I'm really happy for you guys."

"Yeah," Sam said, struggling to breathe normally. "Thanks. Please don't tell anyone else. I can't believe she told you guys."

"Seriously, man," Carter said, sincerity in his voice. "It's not a big deal. I tried to tell you that those three share everything. They talk about our junk constantly."

"Wow," Sam said, besieged by emotion. Betrayal, thick and heavy, coursed through his frame as he resisted the urge to scream. He'd given Joy everything—his love, his body, his trust. How could she divulge his most closely-held secret to anyone, even her closest friends? Inhaling scattered breaths, he conversed with Carter, the words a hazy jumble as he fought to get through the evening. As the event wound down, Joy approached him, threading her arms through her jacket.

"Ready?" she asked, a slight anger in her voice. *She* was pissed at *him*? Fuck that. Sam was livid. As soon as they got home, he was going to confront her, that was for damn sure. She'd betrayed his trust, and for someone who didn't connect easily with people, it hurt him terribly.

They were quiet in the Uber to her apartment, both of them stewing. Sam understood that he'd done something to upset her, but it couldn't be nearly as bad as her breach of trust. They silently rode up the elevator and entered her place, both discarding their jackets and hanging them on the hook by her door. She padded to stand beside the kitchen island, crossing her arms as she regarded him.

Sam closed the distance between them, stopping a few feet in front of her. "I get that you're pissed at me for something, Joy, but I'm pretty fucking angry at you too right now."

"Is that so?" she asked, brows arching. "Because you have a lot of explaining to do."

Lost to confusion about what he could've done that was so heinous, he lifted his arms. "I have no idea what I did. Just tell me."

Slamming her hand on the counter, she lifted a sheet of paper. Holding it high, she wrung it in the air. "Care to tell me about this email from Drake that you had stored on your computer from *four days before I was fired*?" The volume of her voice had risen to a yell and her cheeks were flushed with anger.

Fuck. Sam had completely forgotten about the email he'd screenshotted since his time at RMG seemed like a lifetime ago. "I took that when I was logged in to Drake's computer. I thought it might be prudent at a later date, but wasn't sure how to handle it."

"Hmmm…" she said, smashing it back on the counter before placing her fists on her hips. "Did you think that maybe…I don't know…you'd want to tell me about it?"

Sam lifted his hand, palm facing her. "It's a violation of policy to read employees' personal emails while I'm logged in to their system, Joy. If I'd told you or turned it over to HR, I could've been terminated myself. I wasn't sure what to do, so I let it sit. It was probably the wrong thing to do, and I felt terrible when you were fired. That's why I wanted to offer you the business manager position. I felt like I didn't do enough to prevent your firing and wanted to help you."

"Oh, I see," she said, crossing her arms over her chest. "So, it wasn't because I was great at organizing schedules and a competent executive assistant, as you assured me. It was because you felt guilty."

"No," he said, sighing as he rubbed his eyes with his fingers. "Of course, all of that is true. I just wanted to help you."

"Well, you know what? I don't need you to save me, Sam. I did just fine before I ever got involved with you. And if you really wanted to help me, you would've prevented my termination, but that ship has sailed. At this point, we need to turn this email over to Kevin so he can add it to the evidence. Otherwise, my case against Drake and RMG doesn't have a chance."

"I could get in big trouble if you turn that over, Joy. I violated a ton of policies when I took it. I need to research the implications before you just turn it over to Kevin."

She scoffed. "Of course, you do. I can't believe I trusted you. You're as big of a jerk as Drake."

Fury flooded his system as she stood outraged before him. "You can't believe that *you* trusted *me*?" Taking a step toward her, he jabbed his finger in the air as he spoke. "Imagine my shock tonight when Carter tells me how happy he is that I've finally gotten laid."

Her mouth closed, eyes wide as she stared at him. Her thin shoulders lifted, the movement hesitant, as she said, "He was in the kitchen when I called Kayla and Laura to tell them that we finally hooked up."

"You told them I was a virgin?" Pain threatened to close his throat as he stared into her stunning eyes. "How could you, Joy?

You know how embarrassing that was for me. I can't believe you shared something so personal that should've stayed between us. I never pegged you for someone who could do something like that."

Understanding seemed to permeate her gaze as she studied him. He noticed her throat bob under the skin of her pale neck and wanted to weep with sorrow. They'd both wronged each other terribly and he was suddenly unsure if they could recover. Would he ever have the chance to taste the skin of her sweet neck again? Torn between anger and his intense love for her, he watched her struggle to speak.

"I'm sorry," she said, shaking her head. "I tell Laura and Kayla everything. It didn't even occur to me not to tell them. I don't know what else to say."

"Neither do I," he said, shrugging with frustration. "It seems we have a huge problem here, Joy, and I have no idea how to fix it."

"You can start by giving the screenshot to Kevin," she said, lifting her chin.

He breathed a frustrated laugh. "All you care about is beating Drake. Do you even care that you ripped my heart out tonight? That I'm dying inside knowing you could violate my trust like that?"

"Like this?" she asked, picking up the paper and shaking it. "Because this looks like a pretty fucking huge violation of trust, Sam. Careful throwing stones through glass houses."

Groaning in frustration, he sliced his hand through the air. "I'm not going to stand here and argue with you all night." Stalking to the door, he shrugged on his coat. "Take some time to think about what kind of relationship you want to have here, Joy. I'm not sure if I can ever trust you again."

"Well, I'm not sure if I can ever trust *you* again," she said, arms crossed defiantly.

"Well," he said, shrugging, "then I have no reason to stay. Fuck this." Yanking the door open, he headed into the hallway, slamming it behind him. Numb to what had just occurred, he didn't fully comprehend the situation until he was home, stewing on his couch.

Sitting on the soft cushions, he cursed himself for ever taking that stupid screenshot. What a dumb move. Inhaling deep breaths, he replayed the argument over and over in his mind, searching for a solution. Unfortunately, he admitted that repairing the rift that had been opened by their transgressions against each other would be difficult, if not impossible. And that pretty much sucked, since he was still inexorably in love with Joy.

Chapter 18

Days later, Joy sat on Kayla's couch, sniffling as her friends sat on each side, gently rubbing her upper arms. "You'll be okay, sweetie," Kayla said. "We're going to figure this out."

They'd been having lunch near Kayla's house when Joy had noticed a man at the bar, approximately Sam's height and build, and had burst into tears. Her friends had whisked her to Kayla's apartment, intent that she not have a full-on meltdown in public. Carter had eyed them with trepidation, mumbling that he had lines to practice in the bedroom. Joy would've laughed at his obvious fear of her uncontrollable emotions if she'd had the ability to stop weeping.

"I haven't talked to him in days, guys," she said, blowing her nose. "We just text about his appointments and he's always so short. I think he hates me."

"He doesn't hate you, J," Laura said, swiping her hair from her temple. "He's obviously in love with you. Anyone can tell."

"He said I ripped his heart out," she said, chin wobbling. "I hate that I hurt him, but how could he not think that I'd tell you guys I was his first? I mean, that's so important and it meant so much to me."

"Um, hi," Carter said, padding into the room, palms held up in the air. "Although I want no part of this chick crying fest, I do have something to add here."

"Carter..." Kayla said, a warning in her voice.

"Just hear me out," he said, lowering to sit on the stool that faced the couch. "You three are weird. Like, really fucking weird."

"You're not helping," Kayla muttered.

"Guys don't share everything like you do. I'd never imagined anything like the conversations you guys have until I moved in with Kayla. I mean, how many times can you talk about a guy's junk?"

"Pretty much all day," Laura chimed in.

"Right," Carter said, arching a brow. "Well, that's freaking weird, ladies. I'm sorry, but it is. Sam had no way of knowing you'd tell Kayla and Laura he was a virgin. I know it seems commonplace to you, Joy, because you tell them everything, but I can understand that it was a huge violation of trust for him."

Joy studied him, truly letting his words sink in. "Damnit," she whispered. "I didn't even realize. I'm just so used to telling you all everything."

"I know," Carter said. "And if you explain that to Sam, I think he'll understand that you had no intention of betraying his trust or divulging his secret. I think he'll see that it was really meaningful to you and you wanted to share it with people you love. But you need to explain it to him because he's definitely not going to understand it on his own. I certainly wouldn't. It took me months to comprehend that Kayla discusses every sexual encounter we have with you guys. It's fucking weird, but I'm a stud, so I got over it."

Laughter filled the room as Kayla playfully shrugged. "It's true. You're the best I've ever had, lover."

Standing, he leaned down and kissed her head. "Right back at ya." Smiling at Joy, he said, "You need to tell him, and you need to let go of the email thing. It was a dumb mistake. I can't see Sam doing anything to hurt you. He's probably as messed up as you right now, if not more so. Now, with that, I'll leave you ladies to talk about what a magnificent specimen of masculinity I am and hope you figure this out, Joy."

"Go away," Kayla said, nudging his thigh with her toes. "And, also, thank you." She blew him a kiss as he trailed to the kitchen.

"Damnit, guys," Joy said, running a crumpled tissue under her nose. "I really fucked up."

"Do you love him, honey?" Kayla asked.

"Yes," she said, nodding furiously. "I really, really love him."

"Then you should listen to Carter." Kayla's features scrunched together. "I can't believe I'm saying that, but you should listen to Carter."

"I heard that!" Carter called from the kitchen.

The three of them snickered. Kayla's phone buzzed and she pulled it from her back pocket. Eyes narrowing on the screen, Joy observed her read the email.

"Is everything okay?" Joy asked.

"It's from Kevin," Kayla said, beaming. "Sam turned over the screenshot. Kevin says it will revamp the entire case."

Emotion swept through Joy as she realized Sam had done this for her, even though they hadn't spoken in days. Love for him crashed through her system, her body craving his touch, even if it was just a hug...or a soft caress. God, she missed him so much.

"Kevin said this could have repercussions for Sam, though," Kayla said, scrolling through the email on her phone. "Since he violated the terms of his contract, RMG and Drake could both sue him."

"Crap," Joy said, biting her lip. "I don't want him to be in jeopardy for helping me."

Kayla's brown eyes lifted to hers. "It seems he's willing to chance being sued to ensure you win."

Tears streamed down Joy's cheeks as she digested the information. Sniffling, she wiped her face and sat up on the couch. "I can't let him do this for me. I have to talk to him."

"Oh, my god, it's like a rom-com," Laura said. "Are you going to slow-motion run to his house, declare your love and tell him you'd rather lose the case than have him sacrifice himself?"

Standing, Joy laughed as she nodded to her friends. "That's exactly what I'm going to do. Excuse me, ladies. I have to call a damn Uber."

After hugging them all, and smacking a wet kiss on Carter's cheek, Joy all but skipped from Kayla's apartment, intent on saving the relationship with the man she loved with all her heart.

Chapter 19

S am sat on his couch, laptop open over his crossed legs, going over the books for SamJoy. Noting how impeccable they were, he thought of Joy. He felt terrible that she'd misconstrued his statement about recruiting her, twisting it into some sort of pity play. Instead, she was an integral part of their business and her marketing and organizational skills were paying off tenfold. Fear that she would pack up and leave the business paralyzed him as he absently checked his email.

A message popped up from Kevin, divulging he'd received the screenshot from Sam and had informed Kayla and Joy. Sighing, Sam rested his head on the back of the couch, searching the ceiling for answers, although none were there. After consulting an attorney, Sam understood there could be intense repercussions from sending the info to Kevin, due to his untenable means of obtaining the screenshot, but he just didn't care anymore. If it helped Joy, he would suck it up and take his chances.

Over the past few days, he'd replayed their argument in his head so many times, it now ran on a constant loop. After his anger had dissipated, he thought of Joy's relationship with Kayla and Laura. They were closer than any sisters, any family, he'd ever seen. It made sense Joy told them everything. Being that Kayla lived with Carter, he'd hear everything, if only from proximity.

Joy's face flitted through his mind, causing his eyes to water. Damn, he missed her so much. He wanted to race to her apartment, drag her into his arms and tell her the one thing he should've told her before it all went so horribly wrong.

He should've told her he loved her.

Inescapably, adamantly, unalterably loved her.

The days since their blow up felt like centuries and her texts had been succinct. She was obviously still pissed and he wondered if she'd ever forgive him. How had he managed to screw up the best thing that had ever happened to him? Rubbing his hand over his chest, he let the loss wash over him, more intense than all those years ago when he'd lost his parents.

A knock rapped on the door and his eyes narrowed. Shoving the laptop aside, he strode to the door, pulling it open to see a hesitant Joy on the other side.

"Hey," she said softly. Her eyes were swollen as if she'd been crying, and Sam ached to soothe her.

"Hey," he said, stunned she was at his doorstep.

"Can I come in?"

"Oh," he said, widening the door. "Sure. Sorry."

She stepped through, the scent of her hair attacking his nostrils as he told his pounding heart to calm down. Shrugging off her light coat, she set it on the counter. Appearing nervous, she rubbed her palms over her jean-clad thighs.

"So, I decided it was time we talked. If you're okay with that."

He nodded, unable to speak because his throat was swollen shut. Gesturing to the couch, she trailed over, looking gorgeous in knee-high boots over her jeans and a silky blue top. She moved his laptop toward the coffee table, resting it atop the books scattered there, and lowered to the brown cushions.

"Are you going to sit down?" she asked.

"Sorry," he said, shaking his head. Lowering beside her, he swallowed thickly.

Exhaling a large breath through puffed cheeks, her lips curved into a half-grin. "This is awkward."

"I can start if you want," he said, dying to touch her but terrified she'd pull away.

"No," she said, her gaze falling to her hands, twisting in her lap. "I need to say this." Lifting those limitless blue eyes to his, he noticed they swam with moisture and emotion. "I'm so sorry I divulged your secret, Sam," she said, her voice tender. "I didn't even think about how much it would hurt you if I told Laura and Kayla, and by extension Carter, since he eavesdrops on all our conversations," she rolled her eyes. "It was so stupid and insensitive and I don't blame you if you hate me."

"Joy," he said, shifting to face her and taking her hand. "It's okay. I'm sorry I overreacted."

"You didn't, though," she said, a tear escaping her eye before she swiped it away. "It was a perfectly normal reaction to having your trust violated. I feel awful."

"Don't cry, sweetheart," he said, longing to console her. Cupping her face, he trailed his thumb over the wet track of her tear. "It's okay. I know they're important to you. I understand why you told them."

"They are," she said, sniffling. "Like, really important. They were the most important people in my life until I met you."

Air exited his lungs at her heartfelt statement. "Yeah?"

She nodded. "I know this might be hard to understand, but it didn't occur to me not to tell them. You see, when I experience something amazing and lifechanging, my first instinct is to tell the people I love most. And you certainly changed my life, Sam. I know that being inexperienced was a huge deal to you, but it honestly wasn't for me. What was amazing for me was that you trusted me to be your first. It meant so much to me. It still does. It's one of the many reasons why I love you so much."

Her magnificent face blurred as she stared at him, causing Sam to realize his eyes were burning with tears. "You do?" he asked, his voice gravelly and uncertain.

"So fucking much, Sam. With all my heart. But if you want to take a break, I understand. If you want to try being with other women, I understand. It's not fair for me to expect you to stay with me when I fucked up so badly and you've never really had the opportunity to be with anyone else. I'll give you space if that's what you want. I promise it won't affect my work. We can still be adults about this and we can still build a profitable business."

"Joy—"

"Wait," she said, holding up her hand. "Please let me finish before I lose it, okay?"

He nodded.

Sucking in a breath, she continued. "I don't know how to make this right, but I'm determined to figure it out. And I emailed Kevin on the way over here. I told him not to place Drake's email into evidence. There's no way I'm letting you put yourself in jeopardy like that. We'll forge ahead with what we have and hope it works out. If not, that's fine. I'm over Drake and RMG and all of it. All I want is to move forward."

Happiness infiltrated every pore in his body as he gazed into her eyes. "Are you done?" he asked, arching a brow.

She breathed a laugh. "Yeah. That's all I've got."

Chuckling, he brought his other hand to her face, palming her cheeks as he regarded her so reverently. "Joy," he whispered, unable to control his voice. "Don't you understand that I've loved you since the first day I met you? What the hell is this crap about taking a break? If I had it my way, we'd already be married by now."

She bit her lip, causing his body to tighten with arousal. "I heard you talking with the guys the night you played poker. You seemed to agree with them that only having one lover was quite limiting."

"Oh, god," he said, rolling his eyes. "You heard that? They were annoying the hell out of me. I just told them what they wanted to hear so they'd shut up. How can you think, for one second, that I'd want to be with anyone else but you? I've wanted to tell you so many times how much I love you when you look at me with those stunning eyes while I'm inside your gorgeous body. I've never felt so connected to anyone, Joy. I just didn't want to freak you out with avowals of love you weren't ready to hear."

"I'm ready," she said, sliding her arms around his neck. "I'm so damn ready, Sam. Tell me."

Resting his forehead against hers, he nuzzled the tip of her nose with his. "I love you so much, Joy Paulson. I want to marry you and build a family with you and spend every second I can with you. This is it for me. The day I met you was the first day of the rest of my life."

"Oh, Sam," she said, capturing his lips as she moaned into his mouth. Kissing her with all the desire and love he possessed, he drew her across his lap, loving how she straddled him as her legs slipped around his waist. Breaking the kiss, they held each other, stroking each other's skin, reclaiming what they'd come so close to losing.

"Can we promise we'll never fight like that again?" she asked. "Because that pretty much sucked."

He nipped her lips. "Promise. I can't lose you, Joy. You're everything."

Sighing, she ran her fingers through his hair. "I think you need to show me."

Growling, he rose from the couch, loving how she clung to him as he carried her to the bedroom. Once there, he gently placed her on the comforter, ardently kissing her as he ripped at their clothes.

When she lay beneath him, her skin exposed and silky under his own, Sam wanted to cry with delight. Using every skill he'd learned...everything she'd taught him...he brought them both to the peak of desire before slipping inside her deepest place.

"I missed having you inside me," she said, looking like a sultry goddess as her hair fanned upon the bed.

"Me too," he said, working his hips in a slow, steady pace. "It's where I feel most at home. You're my home, Joy."

A tear escaped her eye and he kissed it away, trailing his lips to rest on the shell of her ear. "I'm going to make you come while I'm inside you."

"I don't think I can," she whispered.

Sliding his hands down, he glided them under her butt, grabbing the luscious globes in his hands. "Cross your ankles behind my back."

She complied, opening her body to him in ways they'd never tried. Gazing into her eyes, he probed her with his shaft, searching for places that were sensitive. Suddenly, she gasped. "Oh, that felt good."

Moving back, he focused all his energy on the tender spot. Undulating his hips, he raked the head of his cock through her sensitive folds, encouraged by her ravaged little sighs.

"Oh, my god," she said, her body tensing under his. "I think you found it. Don't stop. I think I'm going to come." Her head tilted back, eyes drifting closed, as her wet lips opened, her mouth forming an "O".

Dying to please her, he concentrated on stimulating her with the head of his shaft, more focused than he'd ever been during his three decades on the planet. Her gasps became cries, her moans became screams and, suddenly, her back arched and she began to convulse, falling apart in his arms as he loved her. Overcome with emotion at being the man to give her such pleasure, Sam closed his eyes and let go, giving in to his own release.

The walls of her core milked him as he pumped into her, jetting his release inside her sweet body, never wanting to let go. Whispered words of love mingled with exclamations of desire as their sweat-soaked bodies fused into one. Lost in a haze of passion, Sam finally found the strength to lift his head.

"How was that?" he asked, stroking the hair from her forehead.

"Holy shit," she said, lids opening as she grinned from ear to ear. "I've never come that way before. I didn't think it was possible."

"You were an intercourse orgasm virgin," he teased, causing her to laugh.

"I guess I was. We both lost our virginities to each other, in a way."

Chuckling, he nodded. "We did. I'm so honored you're my first lover too, by the way. I can tell it means something to you and that's really special."

"It means so much to me, Sam," she said, trailing her nails over his arm, causing his still-trembling body to shiver. "I'm so sorry I hurt you."

"I'm sorry I hurt you too," he said, placing a soft peck on her lips. "I never should've taken that stupid screenshot, and I should've told you about the email right away. I'm so damn sorry."

"No more apologies," she said, her smile so tender. "But we do need to take this as a lesson to communicate better. I thought we were doing such a great job but I guess we can always improve."

"Yeah," he said, resting his head on his hand as he stroked her collarbone. "We definitely can. And I'm just going to have to accept you're going to tell the girls everything."

She bit her lip, causing his dick to twitch inside her. The action was just too damn adorable. "That's true, I'm afraid. I'd tell you it wasn't, but I don't want to lie to you. But at least you and Carter can band together and make fun of us. I know he's excited to have another guy in the group. We drive him pretty insane, but he deserves it most of the time."

"We'll do our best to put up with you crazy broads," he teased. Tracing his finger over her lips, he whispered, "I love you so much, Joy."

"I love you too," she said, hugging him to her by draping her leg across the back of his thigh.

As their bodies cooled, Sam thanked the heavens she was back in his arms, knowing her love was the most beautiful and precious gift he'd ever received. Determined to build a life and a family with his magnificent Joy, he lost himself in her eyes, and in the anticipation of all they would create together.

Sam, who'd been without a family for so long, was finally home.

Epilogue

S am stood backstage at Carter's play, nerves rampant as he ran his wet palms over his khaki pants.

"You ready, man?" Carter asked.

"Yeah," Sam said. "It's now or never. Do it."

Carter went out to take his bow, the last of the cast since he was the star. As the crowd clapped, he spoke into the microphone he'd carried on stage.

"Well, folks, in honor of Valentine's Day, we have a surprise for you. My buddy, Sam, has something he needs to do and I need you all to support him, okay?"

Cheers and whistles emanated from the crowd.

Carter turned and smiled and Sam felt a warm blanket of contentment surround his slightly-trembling body. Anticipating the look in Joy's eyes, he walked on stage and took the microphone from Carter's hands.

J oy assessed the crowd, wondering why Sam was taking so long in the bathroom. The play was now over and Carter was about to take his bow. She'd purchased several rounds of drinks for the group tonight, thanks to her new settlement from her case against Drake and RMG, so maybe his bladder was extra full or something.

It turned out that having an active sexual harassment lawsuit hadn't been attractive to many of the new clients RMG was actively pursuing, and they had settled the case for several hundred thousand dollars. Sam's screenshotted email wasn't needed to strengthen Joy's case after all, and it had never been admitted into evidence, saving him from any legal consequences. All in all, it was one of many happy endings Joy had experienced since beginning her life with Sam. He was, indubitably, the best thing that had ever happened to her.

"Guys, I think Sam fell in," she joked, searching the theater.

"Oh, I think you'll find him soon enough," Laura said, mischief in her tone.

Joy's eyebrows drew together. "What does that mean?"

"Look, honey," Kayla said, pointing to the stage.

Carter was addressing the crowd, droning on about Valentine's Day, and then Sam walked onto the platform, appearing slightly nervous, with a big, goofy grin on his face. Wait, what was Sam doing onstage? Lifting the microphone, he cleared his throat.

"A year ago today, the woman of my dreams made me the happiest man alive and became my girlfriend," Sam said, his gaze boring into her as she stood in the front row. Several cries of "*awwww*" and "*ohhhh*" filtered through the crowd and Joy didn't even try to stop the tears that welled in her eyes from streaming down her cheeks.

"I'm hoping that this Valentine's Day, a year after we officially became partners, the beautiful and amazing Joy Paulson will do me the honor of becoming my wife." Lowering to his knee, he held up a ring box, a sparkling diamond ring inside.

Joy was frozen with emotion, unable to move until Kayla grabbed her hand and dragged her to the stairs that led to the stage. With heavy feet, she climbed, taking Carter's hand as he helped her up the stairs. He led her over to Sam, winking at her as he whispered in her ear, "Don't blow this, Paulson."

She beamed at him before turning to face Sam, so handsome on one knee as he held up the ring box. "Joy, I love you so much, sweetheart. Will you marry me?"

Clutching her hand over her mouth to contain her sobs, she nodded. "Yes," she croaked, extending her left hand down so he could slide the ring over her finger. As the crowd roared, Sam stood, embracing her and lifting her off the floor as he twirled her around. Joy held on for dear life, kissing him as if his lips were as integral to her as the air she breathed.

And, perhaps, they were.

Feeling her feet hit the ground, she cupped his cheeks. "I can't believe you did this. I would've never thought my shy Sam would propose in front of a theater full of people."

"It's Valentine's Day and I needed to do something extraordinary. This day will always be so special for me, honey."

"For me too," she said, placing a tender kiss on his full lips. "For me too."

The End
(and happy Valentine's Day!)

Acknowledgments

M y acknowledgments for this book are short and sweet. Thanks so much to Aleks, Jaime, Nadine, Hannah, Kat, Laura and Keira for embracing this new venture (and for craving sweet, steamy books like I do!). Your support is truly amazing and I'm eternally grateful.

Before You Go

O kay, awesome readers, how sweet was Sam? *Sigh*. I think it's time for Laura to find love too! You can read Laura's book, **Her Patriotic Prince**, right now!

P lease consider leaving a review on your retailer's site, BookBub and/or Goodreads. Your reviews help spread the word for indie authors so we can keep writing smokin' hot books for you to devour. Thanks so much for reading!

About the Author

Ayla Asher is the pen name for a USA Today bestselling author who writes steamy fantasy romance under a different pseudonym. However, she loves a spicy, fast-paced contemporary romance too! Therefore, she's decided to share some of her contemporary stories, hoping to spread a little joy one HEA at a time. She would love to connect with you on social media, where she enjoys making dorky TikToks, FB/IG posts and steamy book trailers!

ALSO BY AYLA ASHER

Manhattan Holiday Loves Trilogy
Book 1: His Holiday Pact
Book 2: Her Valentine Surprise
Book 3: Her Patriotic Prince

Ardor Creek Series
Book 1: Hearts Reclaimed
Book 2: Illusions Unveiled
Book 3: Desires Uncovered
Book 4: Resolutions Embraced
Book 5: Passions Fulfilled
Book 6: Futures Entwined

Made in the USA
Middletown, DE
14 December 2023